Hot Latin Docs

Sultry, sexy bachelor brothers on the loose!

Santiago, Alejandro, Rafael and Dante Valentino
are Miami's most eligible doctors. Yet the brothers'
dazzling lives hide a darker truth—one that made
these determined bachelors close their hearts to
love years ago…

But now four feisty women are about to turn the
heat up for these sexy Latin docs and tempt them
each to do something they never imagined—
get down on one knee!

Find out what happens in:

Santiago's Convenient Fiancée by Annie O'Neil
January 2017

Alejandro's Sexy Secret by Amy Ruttan
January 2017

Rafael's One Night Bombshell by Tina Beckett
February 2017

Dante's Shock Proposal by Amalie Berlin
February 2017

D0836994

Dear Reader,

I discovered a few wonderful things in the course of writing *Santiago's Convenient Fiancée*. First—new friends don't need to live around the corner to be close! Writing with these *chicas bonitas* was an absolute pleasure.

Another discovery: changing my desktop picture from my dogs to Miami Beach. I live in England and wrote this in the dead of winter, so that visual splash of sunshine, white sand and Art Deco never failed to get my synaptic gaps flashing. And would you believe it? I have never hankered for Latin American food more than during the writing of this book. Rural England is *not* the best place to come across plantains and *puerco pibil*, believe you me.

And finally—writing about a scrumptious Latino with a huge heart and a chip on his shoulder is *deeee*-lightful. Especially with Saoirse Murphy as his heroine. She's the kind of gal I'd just love to be friends with. Loyal, feisty, passionate about her work and fighting with every bone in her body not to fall in love with the most yummy, inky-haired, long-legged, perfect-looking man she has ever seen.

Please, *please* don't be shy. I love hearing from readers—good or bad. I promise I'm working on a thick skin! I can be reached at annie@annieoneilbooks.com or @AnnieONeilBooks on Twitter. Oh! And I'm on Facebook, too.

See you soon—and enjoy!

Annie O' xo

SANTIAGO'S CONVENIENT FIANCÉE

———

ANNIE O'NEIL

HARLEQUIN® MEDICAL ROMANCE™

Recycling programs
for this product may
not exist in your area.

ISBN-13: 978-0-373-21504-1

Santiago's Convenient Fiancée

First North American Publication 2016

Printed in U.S.A.

Books by Annie O'Neil

Harlequin Medical Romance

Christmas Eve Magic
The Nightshift Before Christmas

The Monticello Baby Miracles
One Night, Twin Consequences

The Firefighter to Heal Her Heart
Doctor…to Duchess?
One Night…with Her Boss
London's Most Eligible Doctor

Visit the Author Profile page
at Harlequin.com for more titles.

This book goes unabashedly to the women behind the creation of each of the Valentino brothers— The Ugly Sisters. Tina, Amalie and Amy—you kept the fiery, feisty, sizzlin' hot hearts of each story shining bright and strong. Thank you, ladies— you're in a class of your own (a really good one, in case you didn't know that already). Thanks, too, to the great team at M&B/Harlequin. May there be a Mad Ron margarita in each of your futures. Xx

CHAPTER ONE

SANTI CLENCHED HIS fists so tightly it hurt. Good. There was still feeling in them. He shot his fingers out at full length, simultaneously giving them a hard shake. The movement jettisoned him back to memories he'd thought he'd left back in Afghanistan. Syria. Africa. Wherever. Didn't matter. Dog tags were dog tags. CPR worked or it didn't. The need to shake it off and stay neutral was the same no matter where he was.

What mattered now was the chest in front of him needing another round of compressions. Fatigue couldn't factor into it. Giving this guy another shot at living could.

"Where the hell is the ambulance?" he bellowed to anyone who might be in the vicinity. The only answer…the echo of his own voice reverberating off the cement stanchions of the underpass. Raw. Frustrated.

Santi wove his fingers together again and pressed the heel of his palm to the man's chest, ignoring the worn clothes, the stench of someone who had slept rough too many nights and the fact he'd been providing CPR for twenty minutes since he'd rung for an ambulance.

"C'mon, Miami!" he growled, keeping steady track of the number of compressions before stopping to give the two rescue breaths that just might jump-start this poor guy's system. "Give the man a chance."

He glanced at the man's dog tags again. Diego Gonzalez.

"What's your story, amigo?" He tugged off his motorcycle jacket, leaving it where it fell on the dry earth before beginning compressions again. He might leave it for Diego once the ambulance turned up and they got a shot or two of epi and some life back into him. From the state of Diego's clothes, the world had given up on him. Well, he sure as hell wouldn't. He'd seen it time and again since he'd left the forces. Veterans unable to find a path after their time overseas. Nothing computing anymore. Lives disintegrating into nothing. He might have hung up his camos just a few months ago, but the last thing he was going to do was forget the men who'd given the military their all, only to find life had little to offer when they came home.

Home.

The word was loaded, and just as dangerous as a sniper bullet. He shook his head again, tightening his fingers against his knuckles as he pressed.

Twenty-nine, thirty.

As he bent to give another two breaths he heard the distant wail of a siren.

"Finally."

One. Two. Three...

"Ready or not! Here we come!" Saoirse flicked on the whoop-whoop of the sirens, loving the wail of sound that cleared a path through the thick of Miami's commuter traffic.

"For crying out loud, you mad Irish woman! You're not in your racing car now."

"Is that you angling for a ride this weekend, Joe?" Saoirse grinned.

"I'll be happy to make it through this shift alive, thank you very much. And then you are taking me straight to the cantina. *Safely,*" he added with a meaningful look as she took the next turn at full pelt. "And heaven help your next partner. They're going to need nerves of steel."

Saoirse laughed, weaving between the cars as if she were barrel racing a horse she'd known since it was a colt. Smooth, fluid. It was grace in motion, if weaving an ambulance through grumpy Floridian drivers was your thing. It was hers. Hadn't always been. But speed ran through her blood now and the tropical heat suited her to a T.

At least something in the past year had turned out all right.

Life had well and truly shot her in the foot, but it had also given her a visa to the States. It should have been a fiancée visa, but the student visa did the same trick. Not that the change of direction still wasn't raw. Still too fresh to discuss. She gave her head a quick shake and refocused.

"What kind of cake will you be having, then, Joe? Not that awful rainbow-colored thing you had on your birthday, I hope."

"Hey, little whippersnapper. It's *my* retirement party—not your twelfth birthday."

"I'm partial to coconut." She gave him a cheeky wink, eyes still glued to the traffic. "We don't get that sort of thing in Ireland. Want me to call the desk and tell them it's your favorite?"

Joe pressed his hands to the dashboard of the ambulance as Saoirse hit the brakes then the gas pedals in quick succession as a very expensive-looking convertible whizzed past them, horn blaring.

"What's up with them?"

"They weren't expecting Annie Oakley behind the wheel, Saoirse," Joe hollered. "For the love of my retirement check! You're going to give me a coronary before we get to the call!"

"Joe! What are the chances you're going to pronounce my name properly before our last ever shift is over? Sear-*shuh*." She overexaggerated the vowel-heavy name her parents had lumbered her with. Maybe she should change that, too. Chopping off most of her hair had been downright liberating.

Joe made another mangled attempt at pronouncing it as they lurched through the next junction and Saoirse laughed.

"If I've told you once, I've told you twice, just go with *Murphy*. If that's too much for you, Murph will do just grand."

"Sorry, darlin'." Joe spoke through gritted teeth as they shot through another red light. "I'm of the generation where you do not call a lady by her last name."

"Is that what you think I am?" Saoirse shot him a sidelong glance. "A lady?"

"Well," grumbled her partner of two months, "something like that, anyways."

Saoirse threw back her head and laughed. "Don't you worry, Joe. I'll get you to your party safe and sound tonight. Your wife won't have to worry. There's only one heart attack we're fixing today and that's whoever is…" she abruptly pulled the ambulance to a halt at the side of an overpass where a motorcycle stood without a rider "…under this bridge. You ready for a bit of off-roading?"

"Down here!" Santi shouted as loudly as he could once the siren's wail was turned off in midscreech and he heard the slamming of doors. Keeping count as he took in the change of environment was second nature to him. What wasn't was registering the stuntwoman-style entrance of the paramedic.

The skid down the embankment was more snowboarder with a portable defibrillator than cautious EMT adhering to health and safety codes. First came the boots in a cloud of gravel and dust, then a set of…decidedly female legs…a swoop of a waist and… *Ker-ching!* This woman wore her regulation jumpsuit as if she were delivering a sexy singing telegram. Hard to do, harder to pull off.

"How long you been at it?"

The lilting voice and ultrafeminine figure didn't match the *C'mon, buckaroo, I dare you to say something unprofessional* attitude her face was actively working. Fine. Suited him. He wasn't here to pick up a date.

"Twenty-four minutes. What took you so long?"

"You look like you know what you're doing," she shot back, all the while pulling out the pads to her twelve-lead ECG. "Why haven't you got him back yet?" Her blue eyes sparked with confrontation as she gave a satisfied "Humph!" in response to his lack of one.

Feisty.

"It's a long time to carry out compressions."

"That's very wise for an EMT."

"Paramedic," she snapped, unshouldering her run bag on the ground opposite him and pressing two gloved fingers to Diego's carotid pulse point, eyes glued to his. If this had been a staring contest he would've been happy to stay all day but they had a life to save.

"Are you sure it's been that long or are we just guesstimating?"

"*We've* been timing." His eyes stayed on hers. "Still early days yet." He gave her a look that said *You give up easy,* received a glare in return as she ripped open the man's shirt—all without blinking. Even the sea went cloudy sometimes, but not her blue eyes. They were as clear as could be. Limitless.

Santi refocused on his hands. "He's a vet."

"You, too?"

Wasn't much of a stretch to make the link. One life wasn't worth more than another, but some prodded at your conscience a bit harder.

"Marines." He never gave much more information than that. He nodded toward the unconscious man. "Diego Gonzalez. That's the name on his tags, anyhow. Thirty!" He gave the two breaths as she applied the monitoring pads to the heavily tattooed chest.

"Joe! How're you coming with the AED?" she shouted over her shoulder, a swish of short blond hair following in her wake as she began peppering Santi with questions. "Have you sprayed nitroglycerin, injected epinephrine, anything?"

"Yeah. I keep it just here in my invisible magic bag of tricks."

"Easy there, cowboy. It was just a question."

He checked his tone before he continued. She was just doing her job. He needed to do his.

"I saw him stagger at the side of the road when I was riding past. Then he fell down the embankment. I'm an off-duty doc—paramedic," he quickly corrected. Coming to Miami was about looking forward, not what he'd left behind. "I was on my bike so...no run bag. That's why I called you guys. There are some cuts and bruises that'll need looking at and I'm pretty sure he could do with a saline drip." He nodded down at Diego's dry skin. "Dehydrated. Big time."

"Right. Guess we'd better get to it, then." She raked around in her bag as her partner skidded to the bottom of the hill in a slow-motion version of—what was her name anyway? He hadn't seen her around the depot when he'd checked in to get his schedule. Santi's eyes flicked to her badge.

Murphy.

He gave a satisfied smile. Irish. He'd thought that was what her accent was. Hopefully she'd brought some of that fabled Irish luck along with her, too.

"Open wide, Diego."

Santi watched as she swiftly carried out the

tracheal intubation and attached the airbag and oxygen tanks together. The woman was no stranger to a cardiac arrest. That was for sure.

"Joe! Have you got that AED ready or not? And how about some epinephrine for the poor lad?"

"Give a man a chance, woman!" her partner huffed as he handed over the paddles for the AED unit after he'd pressed the power button. "I'll load you up some epinephrine."

"Thanks, Joe. You're the best tutor a girl could ask for." Her eyes zapped to Santi as the AED began its telltale charging noise. "Are you clear? Wouldn't want you getting shocked, now. Would we?"

He lifted his hands away from Diego's chest and, once again their eyes met. More of a lightning strike than a tiny click of connection. He didn't know what she was seeing in his eyes, but the triumphant glint in hers made his raised hands feel more like a surrender than a safety measure.

"Clear!"

The corners of her lips twitched into a smile at his microscopic flinch. She'd cranked up the volume on purpose. It was easy enough to see she wasn't flirting, but not so simple to put a finger on the rise she was trying to get out of him. The day was pulsing with tropical heat, but this woman didn't sweat. But, *válgame Dios*, did she ever have a glow.

He followed her gaze to the portable heart monitor. Nothing.

"Joe?"

Her colleague wordlessly handed her a syringe loaded with a one-milligram dose of epinephrine as Santi recommenced compressions.

"Want me to get the backboard?" Joe asked with an unenthusiastic glance up the steep embankment. The poor guy looked like he could've done with an iced coffee in the shade. January wasn't usually this hot, but it's what the weather man had brought.

"Don't worry, we don't need it for this phase. Too uncomfortable for the patient while we're doing compressions." Santi threw the guy a get-out-of-hard-labor option. "When I finish this round, why don't you take over compressions and I'll get it—"

"Hey! You'll stay exactly where you are, big shot," Murphy jumped in. "You're not raking round our ambulance. We don't know you from Adam."

"He said he's a paramedic," Joe interjected, obviously still hopeful he wouldn't have to clamber up the embankment. "Who are you with?"

"No one today. I'm what they call in between positions." He saw Murphy's eyes narrow at his words. She didn't need to know he'd already polished his boots in advance of his first day at Seaside Hospital. "Twenty-nine. Thirty."

He raised his hands away from Diego's chest and looked directly into Murphy's eyes as she pressed the charge button on the AED. Through the high-pitched whine of the charging defibrillator he felt an otherworldly surge of electricity hit him in the solar plexus. That indefinable connection that made a man cross a crowded room when his eyes lit on a perfect stranger and the organic laws of chemistry did their explosive best to bring them together. He hadn't felt that charge of attraction in a while. On a roadside, giving CPR to a vet, wasn't exactly where he'd thought he'd feel it next, but...he hadn't really thought there'd be a "next." Too many ducks already waiting to be put in a row. He scraped a tooth along the length of his lower lip, eyes still glued to hers... The hot Miami sun wasn't the only thing warming him up.

And then—she blinked.

Ah...so he wasn't alone here. *She felt it, too.* "Huh."

He heard the sound—an instinctual response to disbelief—come from her throat, but her lips hadn't even parted. Just pushed forward in a disapproving moue that disappeared as she pulled her lips in on themselves and swallowed whatever words were roiling around her mind.

Santi fought his own features, trying to maintain his best neutral face when all he wanted to do was grin.

His first chink in her Gaelic armor.

He wasn't a flirter and this sure as hell wasn't flirting, but—electricity was hard to ignore. The automated voice of the AED broke through the static in his head. Verbal sparring would have to wait. He watched as her eyes flicked to the monitor at the sound of the electric charge making the connection.

A thin flat line.

Her fingers shot down to Diego's carotid artery and, as if she was an angel delivering the healing touch…beep, beep, the flat line re-formed into the graphic mountainscape that was a beating heart. It was a far cry from a match to the Rocky Mountains—more like the rolling hills of South Dakota—but with a bit of luck and a stint in the hospital he'd get there. The triumphant glint returned.

"Guess you'd better get away up that hill for a backboard, then." She jutted her chin toward Joe. "It's my partner's last day. We don't want the old fella slipping a disk or anything, now, do we?"

"Watch it, girlie. I still have plenty of time to file a grievance against you and get you shipped back to where you came from," Joe cautioned, as he all but proved her point by performing the stretch and twist only a stiff back could bring.

A jag of discord took hold of her features and

just as quickly was lifted away with a bright smile. There was a story there. But she hid it well, cleverly tucking it away behind a sharp wit and a winning smile. Miles better than his go-to scowl.

"That'd be about right, Joe. Picking on a poor wee girl fresh off the boat from Ireland. Now, quit your faffing about and get me another dose of epi, would you?"

Santi's eyebrow lifted in an amused arc. At five feet and a splash of something extra, this woman—"Murphy"—would've struggled at a standing-room-only stadium concert. But he had little doubt she was head and shoulders above your average crowd.

"Hey," he asked as he pressed up from the ground, "what's your name, anyway?"

The smile she was refusing to give him morphed into a smirk as she raised a finger and double-tapped her name tag.

Murphy.

So that's all he was getting.

He felt his lips peel into a full smile as he took the steep incline in a few long-legged strides. They'd board up Diego then away she'd go...

Meeting this enigmatic woman was no doubt going to fall into the brief encounter catalog of his life, but he could feel the moment elbowing into the happy memories section. Suffice it to say the department wasn't very big, but the unexpected jolt of affirmation that he was still a red-blooded male was a reminder that some parts of life were definitely worth living.

"Here you are, *mija*."

Saoirse reached out both hands to take the iced glass, loaded to the brim with a freshly whizzed margarita. With salt. It was a take-no-prisoners cocktail and about as well deserved as end-of-day drinks got.

"Your parents named you well, Ángel!" She gave the bartender a grateful smile. It had been a lo-o-o-ng day. New Year's Day celebrations seemed to have lasted two weeks in Miami. One of their patients had only been adorned in a swirl of glittery tinsel. Didn't he know it was bad luck to leave his decorations up so long? Or take quite so many little "magic" pills? It was one way to start the New Year with a bang. His girlfriend had looked exhausted.

"Murph!"

She looked up, scanning the growing crowd, eyes eventually landing on her friend Amanda waving to her from the entryway to the patio, arm crooking in a *get your booty over here now* arc. She took a huge glug of the margarita, convincing herself it was to make sure the drink didn't spill as she wove her way through Mad Ron's Cantina to the picnic-table-filled, blue-tiled garden area already overflowing with well-wishers for Joe. She'd been lucky when she'd landed him as a mentor in her work-study program. The guy had seen it all. Not to mention the fact that, forty years on, an ambulance had helped him accrue a vast pool of friends. The place was heaving.

"Hey, girl! What took you so long?" Amanda gave her one of those American half hug things she was growing to like. Irish people weren't huggy like this, but after the day… No. Make that the *year* she'd had? The blossoming friendship was a much-needed soul salve.

"I wanted to stop by the hospital to check on a patient."

"Oh? Bit of a hottie, was he?"

Saoirse snorted. Mostly to cover up the fact it had been the roadside stranger she'd been hoping to see, not the tattoo-covered vet they'd saved.

"Not so much. But he'd been out a long time— cardiac arrest—and I wanted to see what his recovery was like. Curiosity. Never seen a guy make it through who'd had over twenty minutes of compressions."

"You did that? Twenty minutes?" She blew on her fingers in a color-me-impressed move.

"Don't be mad!" Saoirse waved away the suggestion, trying to shake the mental image of Mr. Mysterioso's very fine forearms as she did. She had a thing for forearms and his had launched straight to Number One on the Forearms of the

Week list. Not that she actually kept a list or anything. She blinked away the image and forced herself to focus on Amanda. "No mad compressions for me. I would've stuck my magic electric shockers on him straight away." She made her best crazed-scientist face to prove it was true.

"You're such a diligent little paramedic, aren't you?" The verbal gibe was accompanied by an elbow in the ribs.

Saoirse jabbed her back and laughed. "Hey! Don't be shortist!"

"As long as you promise not to be tallist!"

They clinked glasses with a satisfying guffaw. Amanda towered over Saoirse and rarely missed a moment to comment on her friend's diminutive stature. Just about the only person in the world who could.

A swift jab of pain shot through her heart at the memory of her fiancé—ex! Ex, ex, *ex*! Ex-fiancé resting his head on top of hers. To think it had made her feel safe! What a sucker. She shook off the scowl the memory elicited and replaced it with a goofy smile when she saw Amanda's questioning look. The woman had laser vision right into her soul. "Wouldn't it just be my luck to come across the lippiest desk nurse in the whole of Miami?"

"Not everyone's prepared to take all your blarney, Murph. Fess up. Why were you really at the hospital? Don't tell me you're a margarita behind the rest of us just because of quizzical interest. You got exams coming up or something?"

Saoirse avoided the light-saber gaze her friend was shooting at her and took another thirst-quenching glug, a shiver juddering through her as the ice hit her system.

"Oh. My. Word." Amanda's eyes were well and truly cemented across the heaving garden. Saoirse's shoulders dropped. Phew. Dodged a bullet. Looked like eye candy had saved the day.

"Three o'clock," Amanda murmured. "Tall, dark and too freakin' sexy for the word sexy. I'm going to get a cavity in my eye from the sweetness of this man. Murph—what's better than sexy?"

Mr. Mysterioso popped into her head and quite a few words jostled for pole position. "Edible? Scrumptious? Lip-lickingly perfect? Luscious?"

Hmm...there was a bit of a food theme going on here. Couldn't have anything to do with the perfect caramel color of the knight in shining motorcycle gear's forearms, could it?

"Luscious," Amanda repeated, her voice all soft and swoony. Was she remembering she was happily married?

"Three o'clock?" Saoirse had to at least take a glimpse. Looking never hurt, right? It was the *feeling* part that hurt—and she wouldn't go down that stupid, heart-crushing path again.

Her eyes flitted from face to face, none of

them fitting into the knee-weakening territory Amanda's stranger clearly dominated. "I can't see him!"

"Get up on the picnic bench, then." Amanda didn't wait for Saoirse to protest, all but lifting her up and aiming her toward the entryway. "You've got to get a look. This guy could fill up a calendar all by his lonesome. Then they'd have to make up some more months just for fun... Can you imagine it? Mr. Yes-Ma'am-uary!" She gave a military salute before giving Saoirse an additional prod to hurry her up on her quest to steady herself on the bench seat.

"For crying out loud, Amanda. Quit your pushing, will you? I can get on the bench by myself— Oh..."

They said lightning never struck twice. But that had been disproved. And today was blasting another hole in the theory.

"You see what I mean?"

Did she ever? And when Saoirse's eyes connected with the object of their evaluation...she needed to get down from the bench. Quick smart.

"He's all right. I've seen better." Saoirse jumped down and took another spine-juddering slurp of her icy drink. Her jets needed cooling. Big time.

"You've gone mental." Amanda's jaw all but dropped in disbelief. "The man rocks it!"

"Rocks what exactly?" Saoirse went for a dismissive snort and ended up cough-choking. *Awesomely sexy.* Not.

Okay. So she didn't really need to ask the question because she knew exactly what he rocked. And it wasn't just her boat. He was rocking her tummy. Which was currently doing some sort of loopy ribbon-twirling fest thing with the half of margarita it had inside it. He was rocking her heart. Which seemed to have kicked up a notch—or seventeen—in the pace department. Her entire nervous system was experiencing a takeover as if he were playing a goose-bump xylophone along her arms...then down her back and in a sort of heated swirl around her—

"Uh." Amanda pressed a hand to her friend's forehead. "Are you sure you weren't at the hospital to make sure you aren't going clinically *insane*?" She drew out the last word just to make super sure Saoirse knew her friend thought she was nuts. "How on earth are we ever going to find you a hot boyfriend to marry in the next two months if your taste in men is so weird as to not find that amazing specimen of a man...?" Her hand shot out in a pointy gesture and made contact. With a chest. A chest Saoirse had already had the good fortune to stare at for some length of time earlier that day.

Amanda's jaw dropped again.

"Miss Murphy. We meet again."

CHAPTER TWO

YOU *KNOW* HIM?

That's what Amanda's wide-eyed look said. And then she said it out loud for good measure.

"Ha!" Saoirse barked. "No."

Saoirse's eyes darted between her friend and Mr. Mysterioso. *This was awkward.* Why wasn't the earth being kindly for once and swallowing her up in a freak sinkhole incident? Now would be a pretty good time for Mother Nature to intervene if she was ever going to show her largesse. She hadn't bothered when her fiancé had left her standing at the altar like a complete and utter ninny in a ridiculous meringue of a dress... Well...it *had* rained a lot so it had masked the tears, but *Hop to it Mummy Nature—now's your chance to make things right!*

"Santiago."

He stretched his hand forward toward Saoirse, who ignored it, and then to Amanda, who—after exclaiming how fun it was that he was a lefty—took it, gave it a stroke with her other hand to check for a ring and shook it in slow motion, all the while mouthing to Saoirse "You know him?"

"Santi, if Santiago's too much of a mouthful."

The comment was aimed directly at her. And elicited some images that would've sent a nun straight to the burning flames place.

Saoirse drained her glass. It wasn't ladylike and rocketed a brain freeze straight to the neurotransmitters that would've helped her with witty rebuttals, but…tough. Mr. Created-for-Calendars here had made an impact and she'd been working long and hard on the impenetrable fortress built around her heart, not to mention her—ahem—golden triangle. Or whatever it was called these days. For crying out loud! It was feeling a bit too much like there was some sort of fireworks display going off in her heavily ignored girlie parts.

"And you are…?"

She could hear Santiago speaking again. Santi-*ahhhh*-go… Of course he'd have a gorgeous name to go with his gorgeous everything else.

Why couldn't she *speak*?

"I'm Amanda and Miss Mutey-Pants here is Sear-*shuh*." Amanda valiantly stepped into the fray with a perfect mimic of Saoirse trying for the billionth time to get people to pronounce her Gaelic name properly. It wasn't that hard. And right now she wished she could tell her friend it was actually pronounced Sear-*shut up, Amanda*!

Santiago turned the full beam of his smile onto Saoirse, clearly enjoying her very obvious discomfort. And that wasn't just the fact she had to tip her chin way up to meet his amused grin. It had been a right old comedy of errors when the pair of them had boarded up Diego and tried to get him up the embankment to the ambulance.

"You all right after this afternoon's workout?"

Oh! It appears someone does a little bit of mind reading on the side.

"I think it'll be safe to say Joe is more than happy to be throwing in the towel today."

"You held your own."

Flatterer.

"What? Coming up on the rear, with you pulling him up one-handed like? I don't think so." She might not want to like him, but the man deserved all the credit on that one. Diego would be wearing a toe tag in the morgue right now if Santiago hadn't swooped in to the rescue. There weren't many folk who would leap off their motorcycles—and, yes, she'd ogled the mint condition road bike, envied it and just for a teensy-tiny second imagined Santiago straddling it—all to come to the aid of a man who most of the world had forgotten about. There was definitely a heart somewhere underneath that big expanse of a chest that was working the plain black T-shirt he was wearing. She tipped her chin to the side as if it would help her see him in a white shirt.

Yup! That would look nice, too. Caramel skin rocked all colors of the just-the-right-amount-of-tight T-shirt world.

"We got there in the end." Santiago's eyes didn't leave her, one of his teeth dragging across his full lower lip in slow motion...just as it had earlier in the day when she'd been very obviously staring at his...er...attributes.

Stop staring at his lips. You are no longer in the kissing business.

Saoirse feigned a "whatever" eye roll just to pull her eyes away from his mouth and ended up stopping in midroll when his dark-lashed eyes caught her own with a teasing wink. He knew her game. She could feel it straight down to her tightly laced mental bodice.

"Saoirse's name means liberty," Amanda quipped, clearly feeling left out of the staring contest.

"And justice to all?" Santiago asked, his eyes taking a quick side trip to Amanda then straight back to Saoirse's, all the while doing their jolly best to unnerve her.

For all the flaming rainbows in Ireland. Were those flecks of *gold* in his coffee-brown eyes? *Nah...* Had to be all the fairy lights laced around the walled patio's palm trees. No one had gold flecks in their eyes. Except for tigers. And lions. Best leave the bears out of it because there was nothing grizzly about the man standing in front of her, waiting for a response to his clever quip.

"I told you. It's *Murphy*. Murph if you get tired halfway through."

She received a lightly arced eyebrow and a suggestion of a smile in response.

Why did everything they said to each other seem to have a sexy, satin-sheets connotation? She briskly turned to Amanda. "I need a drink. Shall I get you anything when I'm at the bar?"

"Same again." Amanda wiggled her near-empty margarita glass, delighted to have a little me time with Mr. Luscious. Saoirse hesitated for a second. Happily married herself, Amanda had matchmaking down to a fine art. Especially given Saoirse's...how to put this exactly...little bitty visa problem. The one she didn't really want to think about ever but had to, given the high-speed tick-tock of that old life clock. Her advanced work-study degree to shift from NICU nurse to paramedic was running out and just thinking about heading back to Ireland turned her palms clammy.

Even so...she gave Santiago a sidelong glance. Poor mite. He wouldn't know what had hit him. Give Amanda five minutes alone with a man and she would have the rest of his life planned out, whether he saw it coming or not.

Ping!

Mr. Luscious blinked.

Uh-oh.

Had they just done that connect-eyes, mind reading thing again?

"How 'bout I give you a hand? The crowd's pretty wild in there." Santiago turned to join her, much to Amanda's delight.

"I'm all right, thanks." Saoirse bristled. Talk about a rock and a hard place. She might be short but she wasn't some helpless female who needed a big strong man to help her carry a couple of drinks. On the other hand, if she left him alone with Amanda it was highly likely they'd find themselves hand in hand on the beach, their bare feet being lapped by the waves as some new age minister united them in eternal marital harmony. She shrugged. This was pretty much a no-win situation. "Do what you like."

"We'll all come!" Amanda hooked her arms through each of theirs as if she were Dorothy and they were all going to gaily skip off on a grand adventure, conquering evil and learning some valuable lessons about themselves along the way.

The only delight at the end of this particular rainbow was going to be another margarita.

"Let's just hope these were worth waiting for. Made by the man himself." Santi handed over the icy goblet.

"Ángel?"

Saoirse's smile broadened for the first time

since her friend had made a flimsy excuse to go
and speak with someone else. "Work matters."
He knew a setup when he saw one. Not that he
minded. Saoirse was ticking a lot of boxes he
hadn't realized needed ticking: Unimpressed.
Funny. Intelligent. Pixie-sexy. He'd never thought
he had a type, but…the length of time it took to
finish a margarita would be time well spent. And
then he'd move on. Like he always did.

"Mad Ron," Santiago corrected with gravitas,
body blocking a couple of people trying to get to
the bar so he could hand Saoirse her fresh drink.

He watched as she took the glass with a rev-
erent nod.

A Mad Ron Margarita. He hadn't had one for
years. 'Twas a thing to be cherished.

She took a slow sip, closed her eyes, the thick
goblet resting against the pink of her lower lip,
and tipped her head back, visibly enjoying the
sensation of the citrusy drink sliding down her
throat. The tip of her tongue slipped out between
her lips and added a bit of salt to the mix. Salsa
music was pumping through the bar, but he was
pretty sure he heard a little moan of pleasure
vibrate along the length of her delicate throat.
Halfway through the motion, he realized he had
licked his own lips in response. He hooked a
thumb in the belt buckle of his jeans and cleared
his throat. *Ojos de ángel.*

"Someone looks like they needed a drink."

"I'm not one to drown my sorrows," Saoirse said with a hint of a prim edge to her voice, "but I am losing an amazing partner today."

"Joe?" He stated the obvious, but scintillating comebacks were eluding him.

"The one and only." She lifted up her glass to toast her invisible partner, who was no doubt holding court in one of the huge semicircular leather banquettes. "I presume that's why you're here."

He gave a vague nod. "Joe mentioned the party when we were loading up Diego." *To Saoirse, but that made it public information, right?*

She didn't need to know he was psyching himself up to do some long overdue bridge building. Mad Ron's wasn't much more than a stone's throw away from the family's bodega and for some reason he'd gotten it into his head that a sighting of Saoirse would strengthen his resolve. Something—or someone—to strengthen the desire to stay in his hometown long enough to make amends. He'd flown back before—on leave—and not even made it this far. It was time he did more than drive by.

"What's your story, then?" He needed to shift focus off of himself. "You're a long way from home."

"Yeah." She scanned the room, a twist of anxiety tugging at the edges of her blue eyes. The girl didn't give up information freely. Woman, rather. There wasn't a curve on her he wasn't itching to caress. But she didn't seem the type for a cheap alleyway make-out session and he was the last person on earth to offer himself up as relationship material. All the more reason to keep his hands to himself.

"Miami suits you."

One of her eyebrows lifted imperiously while the rest of her facial features tried their best not to overtly dismiss him.

He could've chewed the words up and spat them out in the gutter. Ridiculous space fillers. One roadside rescue and a margarita's worth of time with this woman and it was easy enough to ascertain she wasn't a thing like the *pata sucia* he'd grown up with. Dedicated clubbers who regularly saw dawn from the wrong end of the day. There was no lip liner or gloss that could improve on this woman's mouth, let alone any of her other features. A natural beauty.

"What makes you say Miami suits me?" she finally asked. "You think I look like a snowbird, do you?"

"Hardly." He laughed appreciatively. "I think we can safely say I wasn't likening you to a geriatric. However long you've been here in Miami, it seems to have rubbed off on you. *In a nice way*," he emphasized, smiling as her eyes skittered off again in a vain attempt to find her long-gone friend.

He couldn't help himself. As much as the crowded bar would allow, he took advantage of her divided attention to take a luxurious head-to-toe scan of her tomboyish ensemble. Blond hair gone nearly white with the sun. Half pixie, half mermaid, he was guessing by the bikini tan lines ribboning across her collarbones. Sun-kissed shoulders. A bit freckled. Her body-skimming T-backed tank top swept along the curve of her waist. That was all he could make out as the rest of her curves were mostly hidden by a baggy over-alls dress thingy. Something a girl who wasn't on the lookout for a boyfriend would wear. Even so, the shortish skirt showed off a pair of athletic legs. Flip-flops rather than heels. No surprise there. He had his own stash of flip-flops. They were de rigueur in Miami. Her toenails were painted an unforgiving jet black. *Interesting.* Her natural coloring would've suited pastels to a T. It was almost as if she was fighting her own, very feminine, genetic makeup.

"Stop your gawking, would you?" she muttered, flip-flopped feet shifting uncomfortably as the crowd jostled and moved around them. "I'm not so good at taking all these American compliments."

He threw back his head and laughed. "That was an American compliment, was it? What would an Irish person say?"

"Oh…" She ran a finger along her full bottom lip as she thought and for the second time that night Santi felt envious. It was too easy to imagine using his own finger taking that journey, lips descending on hers to explore and taste, salt, lime— *Focus. F-O-C-U-S*.

"They probably wouldn't say anything nice at all," she said with a huge grin. "Just something dispirited about the weather. 'The rain's not rotted your boots yet, then?' Or, 'What on God's green earth have you done, moving to Ireland when you've got the whole of America and the sunshine and the crunchy peanut butter and heaven knows what else when all we've got is too much poetry about getting in the peat before the rains set in and not a single pot of gold at the end of one of blessed rainbow…'"

Her eyes caught with his. The sharp shock of connection hit him again. A connection Saoirse broke so quickly he wondered for an instant if he'd imagined it. Her eyes were so alive, Santi felt he could practically see the memories of her homeland hit her one by one until…hmm…a not-so-nice memory clouded the rest of the good ones out. Pity. She all but lit up from within when she smiled.

"You know—" he tried to give her an out "—they say one of the true tests of becoming a local is surviving a hurricane. Have you been here long enough to go through a season?" He cringed at his own lack of finesse. This was a massive flunk-out in the charm-the-flip-flops-off-the-lady school of making a good impression. He near enough checked his T-shirt for a pocket guard and a row of tidily stashed writing utensils.

"Arrived in the middle of one," she shot back triumphantly, blissfully unaware of his internal fistfight. "The plane nearly had to be diverted."

"But you obviously made it through the storm."

"Something like that."

Another cloud of emotion colored the pure sea blue of her eyes.

And...three strikes...you're out!

Her tone said what her eyes had already told him. They were done now.

She raised her glass with a thanks-for-the-drink lift of the chin. No words necessary for that universal gesture.

See you later, pal. Better luck next time.

And then she disappeared into the thick of the crowd.

Santi looked down at his own drink, considered taking it down in one, but thought better of it. He didn't want to reek of booze the first time he spoke to his brothers in... he looked at his watch to tot up the years that had passed since he'd last spoken to them, proof his brain was all but addled by his run-in with the Irish Rose of Miami Beach.

Right. He put the unfinished drink down on the bar. It was time to do this thing.

He went out to the street and pulled on his half helmet. The one that let in the wind and the scent of the sea as he rode along the causeways to the Keys. It was his go-to journey when he needed to think and he'd been to the Keys and back more times than you could shake a stick since he'd returned to the States four months ago. He'd flown into Boston for no good reason at all. Putting off the inevitable, most likely. If he was going to do this, he wanted to do it right. Fixing fifteen years of messed-up family history wasn't going to happen overnight. He looked up at the evening sky as if it held the answer to his unspoken question. What made reconnecting with family so hard?

He swung his leg over his bike, the strong thrust of his foot bringing the Beast to life with a satisfying roar of the engine. The Beast and he had steadily worked their way down the coast, picking up paramedic shifts here and there as he went. He could've walked straight into any ER he chose after all the frontline doctoring conflict zone after conflict zone had demanded of him. But "downgrading" to a paramedic had fit right. He wanted the raw immediacy being first on the scene required. A penance for everything he hadn't set right when he should've.

What kind of man abandoned his kid brother when he needed him the most? Left his older brothers in the lurch when they'd been doing the best they could with a bad situation?

A boy who'd been loaded with too much responsibility? Or a plain old coward?

Time to see if a decade-plus of being a Marine had made an actual man out of him.

He shifted gears again and headed toward Little Heliconia. The neighborhood he'd been born and raised in held more of his demons than anywhere else in the world. And he'd seen some hellholes in his time.

Santi reached the familiar corner, leather boots connecting with the ground as he debated whether or not to make the turn. A horn sounded behind him and he fought the urge to kickstand his bike and give the impatient driver a little lesson in common courtesy. Waiting two seconds wasn't going to kill anyone. His heart caught for a moment.

At least, not in this scenario.

He sucked in a deep breath, flicked on his blinker and took his bike into a low dip, knee stopping just shy of the asphalt as he rounded the corner.

The lights were on in the back alleyway, but he couldn't see anyone. He turned off the ignition a couple of doors down from the one he knew like the back of his hand, pulled off his helmet and let the night sounds settle around him. The chirrup of tree frogs and steady hum of the crickets kept cadence with the wash and ebb of the waves just a couple of blocks away, but the thud and thump of his heart won out. He'd driven past about twenty times since he'd been back. This was the first time he'd stopped.

"Ay! Dante! Don't forget to put orange soda on the list this time, *pero*. We're out."

Santi's spine stiffened as he heard his older brother give the admonishment. Rafe's words had always held more bark than bite and it didn't look like much had changed. The sound of his voice transported him right back to the time and place when everything had changed. He couldn't even remember why they'd all been in the shop. There had been nothing unusual in it. But the command to get down on the ground had been a first. In less than a minute the "perfect family" had been irrevocably altered.

"Not my fault this time, Rafe. Blame it on *la fea*!"

Santi stifled a guffaw. Still calling each other "the ugly one," were they?

"You boys! Stop your bickering and get back to work. I don't want to be here all night."

"Don't worry, Carmelita. We'll get you back home in time for your favorite soaps."

"No seas tonto," Carmelita shot back, appearing at the back doorway as she spoke over her shoulder. "I know how to record things now on my thingamajig. I'm every bit as modern as you

boys." She cracked a small area rug out into the empty space of the alley, a cloud of dust left billowing in the pool of streetlight with barely a chance to settle before she was in and out of the doorway with another one. Her efficiency had seen them through the darkest days of their lives. She may not have been blood—but she was all the family they'd had after that day.

"Carmelita, give me those. I can finish up."

Santi froze when his little brother appeared alongside their adoptive auntie, then he slowly leaned back on the seat of his bike as if the darkness could envelop him more than it already had.

Carmelita clasped Alejandro's stubbled chin in one of her chubby hands and gave it a loving shake, then patted his cheek as if he were a toddler. "You're a good boy, Alejandro, but I'm not an old woman yet. You already work too hard at that hospital of yours. All of you boys do."

Alejandro clucked away her talking-to and wordlessly took the next mat and gave it a sharp shake.

Santi felt a sting hit him at the back of his throat. His lungs constricted against the strain of trying to swallow back the sour twist of emotion fighting to get out.

Alejandro had changed. Hardly surprising given the last time Santi had seen him he'd been in his midteens. His little brother was a man now. About the same height—six feet with an inch or two more for good measure. He'd been a good-looking kid and the same held true about the man standing not twenty yards away. No thanks to him. He'd bailed when his brother had needed him most. And from the looks of things, he'd done more than all right without him.

Santi swore softly, then swore again when Alejandro turned at the sound.

No. He couldn't do this. Not tonight. Still too soon.

His body went into automatic pilot, turning the key, kick-starting the bike into a roar of disparate sounds that melded into one. The engine, the quick-fire gear changes and the piercing screech of rubber twisting on tarmac couldn't drown out his thoughts as he took the sharp turn out of the alley and without a second's hesitation headed to the bridges so he could hit the Keys and get himself straight again.

CHAPTER THREE

"STOP KICKING THE desk already! What's it ever done to you?"

Amanda smiled as she told her friend off and Saoirse pulled back her booted foot just as it was ready to connect with the ER check-in desk for another thud.

"I'm tired of waiting. Where is this guy anyhow?"

"Ah!" Amanda's eyes lit up and she leaned conspiratorially across the counter. "It's a *male* person, is it? Do you know if he's single? I can't believe you didn't talk to that guy at Joe's going-away party. *Muy guapo*. They don't make them that handsome and available all that often, Murph. You should've pounced." She did her best cat-pounce look, managing to look completely adorable in the process.

"Enough! I'll figure out my little problem outside work hours, thank you very much." She pursed her lips and gave her friend a wide-eyed glare.

"I'm just saying, beggars can't be choosers and you had an amazing option last night..." Amanda paused for effect. "Until you bailed."

"I didn't bail!" *What's so bad about bailing when all you have to offer is yourself? The self her ex couldn't see fit to marry...on their wedding day.*

"And I'm no beggar," she tacked on for good measure—as if it would make a grain of salt's worth of difference to Amanda.

"Yeah, right. Tell it to the deportation police." Amanda pulled out her phone and scrolled through the images until she hit the one she wanted and turned it toward Saoirse.

The calendar. As if she needed a visual aid to remind her the days were passing faster than the sands of time. Or were those the same thing?

"Three months, Murph. Three months to find some talent who is going to put a ring on that finger by the end of your course."

"I told you, I'm not in the market for a ring. Or a romance. None of that. It's a green card I'm after. Nothing more."

"C'mon." Her friend nudged her over the countertop. "If you're going to marry someone so you can stay, he might as well be nice to look at and, come to think of it, there is plenty of talent right here at Seaside. Why not keep it in the family?"

"All right! I get it!" Saoirse cut her off. "I've got more than enough to worry about with having to add Finding a Hottie Who Will Marry the Poor Immigrant Girl whose fiancé couldn't be bothered to do the trick, don't I?"

"Like what, exactly?" Amanda asked pointedly. "What is it you have to worry about besides that?"

"Uh…like my new partner showing up so we can get out of here and fix some people!"

"Amanda." A man's voice cut across Saoirse's. "Know anything about the head injury in cubicle three?"

"Yes, Dr. Valentino. She's just been brought in…"

Amanda's voice turned into a buzz in Saoirse's head as she looked at the doctor standing beside her. He definitely had Latino blood running through him. The smokin' hot variety. Tall, dark hair. Not as pitch-black as Santi's. And the cut was crisp and clean—it would've suited a high-powered businessman just as well as a… What was this guy? Some sort of specialist? Something exacting anyway. The man couldn't have been more alpha male if he tried. Not her type. He wasn't as rakishly *rebel with a cause* as Santi came across with his long lean body all casual and taut at the same time. And that thick, soft ebony hair gently curling along his neck. Not that she'd been burning the details of their encounter into her mind or anything.

She tamped down the memory and tried to

pull a surreptitious sidelong glance at the immaculately dressed interloper. This chap was more gentleman than gaucho in the looks department. He had the same broad-shouldered, athletic build as her guy. Well, not *her* guy but... she knew what she meant. Dark brown eyes, the same rich voice that could've doubled for Spanish hot chocolate...

Her gaze swung to the double doors, opening automatically as a virtual replica of the man beside her purposefully strode in. The closer he got the more prominent the differences became but even so—these two were cut from the same cloth. A very familiar Latino islander cloth if she wasn't mistaken... Caramel-colored skin, cheekbones to die for, dark eyes that could stand in for a shot of spicy mole sauce or espresso, depending on the lighting... She was tempted to go up on tiptoe and look for flecks of gold.

"Amanda, what sort of riffraff are you letting into your ER these days?" he intoned, simultaneously doing the very male chin jut thing to the nearer Identi-Kit doctor. "Rafe! Come over here, I need to pick your brains," he called across the crowded waiting room.

"Two Valentinos are better than one!" Amanda riposted with a cheeky grin, managing, as she handed a chart to him, to eye-signal to Saoirse that both men were ring-free.

Oh, for heaven's sake! Saoirse shifted a heavy-lidded glance at the two gorgeous clones now deep in conversation over the contents of the chart. Amanda, on the other hand, was looking a bit too innocent. There was little doubt her friend was going a bit haywire on this whole let's-find-Saoirse-a-husband-so-she-can-stay thing. There were other options, but maddeningly getting married was the easiest. Nothing like a bit of bureaucracy to kick a girl when she's down. But at least Amanda was trying, which was more than she could say for herself. It was little wonder her godsend of a friend's phone didn't have smoke coming out of it from all of the texts she must've been sending to gather this collection of fine male specimens about the main desk.

Not that they were paying even the slightest bit of attention to her.

Which stung a little.

Okay, more than a little.

This was more than life playing funny jokes on her. This was life being mean. These men were born for procreating. The strong features, the chiseled good looks, the cover-model perfection so many aspired to, only to stumble at the first hurdle. And they were both *doctors*. Smart ones, from the sound of their rapid-fire conversation, huge polysyllabic words effortlessly whizzing between them. These men were meant to have offspring populating the earth, making it a better place. A better place to look at anyhow.

Baby-making.

The words sank to the pit of her stomach like a bad plate of enchiladas.

The one thing she wasn't able to do—and now she was all but fenced in with available men in unspeakably perfect packages?

She tugged at the collar of her uniform as if it would release her from the suffocating thoughts. This was bonkers. As if yesterday's run-in with Mr. Luscious hadn't been cruel enough, life was serving up not one but two variations on the man who'd unwittingly kept her up half the night when what she'd really needed had been a good sleep before she met her new partner, who would no doubt make her day a misery by not having the slightest clue—

Her eyes widened as the main character in her nocturnal reflections stepped through the sliding glass doors and into the ER. His eyes scanned the large waiting room before locking with hers, a smile lighting up his face at the hit of recognition. His gaze shifted to her left and then again to her right. One second for each of the doctors flanking her before he executed an abrupt about-face and walked straight back out to the ambulance bay.

Saoirse took off at a run to catch up with him, vaguely hearing Amanda shouting something about her paperwork. The backpack stuffed in her locker would have to wait. The chances of her having a ring on her finger by the end of the month were looking less and less likely. Right now she just needed to make sure she kept her job. On the brink of deportation *and* homelessness wasn't an option.

"Hey!" she shouted when she'd swerved past her ambulance and had caught up with Santi. "What's your problem?"

"I could ask you the same thing." He whirled around to face her, hands on hips, body poised as if ready to pounce if she came any closer.

"What are you talking about?"

"Why were they there with you?"

"What? Who? Are you talking about those guys? The Mirror Men?" She threw a look back over her shoulder as if they would magically appear.

"You don't know them?" Santi was looking at her with an intensity that, frankly, was a bit unsettling. She'd endured quite enough inspection and being unsettled to last her a lifetime, thank you very much. She glared back. Her eyes widened suddenly as her brain started connecting a whole bunch of dots she hadn't seen sixty seconds ago.

Santi was wearing a uniform. The same one she was.

"Are you here to work on Ambulance 23?"

"Yes. How did you know that?"

Oh, for the love of Pete!

"You're kidding, right?"

He shook his head. "I don't know what you're talking about."

"Yeah, right."

Amanda was going to get a very long, very shouty text message coming her way. Saoirse tapped her name tag in a repeat of yesterday's gesture. "Ring any bells?"

This time Santi's eyes did the widening. "They didn't give me a name. Just the number of the vehicle." He rocked back on his heels, deliciously toned forearms folding across his chest as his frown deepened. "You're my new partner?"

"Well, don't bother sounding pleased about it or anything," she snapped back, more angry at her meddling friend whose brainchild she supposed this was than the unwitting hottie she had to sit next to all day. There was no way Amanda wasn't involved in the pairing. It was taking the whole matchmaking thing one step too far. Amanda knew everything about the past year was still stinging as badly as if Saoirse'd just rolled in nettles. Pain lurked in every nook and cranny she possessed. There would be words. Terse ones.

She pursed her lips and gave a heavy sigh. Fine. They might as well get this over with.

She pulled the keys from her pocket and gave them a jangle. Santi reached for them and she pulled them away before he could grab them. "Uh-uh! I drive. Them's the rules."

"I thought I was meant to be senior."

"Not on this rig."

Santi laughed. "Look at you, talking all tough."

The words sobered Saoirse up instantly. "I am tough." She nodded a short, sharp, don't-even-try-to-mess-with-me nod at him. "You're meant to advise me if you feel it's necessary, and I'm telling you right now, it won't be necessary."

He nodded.

"Let's get going, shall we? You're late and I need to run you through everything in the truck before we go anywhere."

"Yes, ma'am." He gave her a sharp salute.

"I'm not screwing around." She gritted her teeth to stop a whole mess of impolite images his faux obedience elicited. A riding crop might've been one of them. And a nonregulation issue nurse's outfit. Neither matched the other, but neither did she and this...this...übermale slanting a dubious eyebrow in her direction.

"Neither am I." One look up into those eyes of his told her Santiago was serious. Very. "Do you want to continue this display of who's more important than who or should we just get to work?"

Turning around and getting into the cab of the ambulance was her only option. With a little bit of slamming.

Damn, that man pressed a whole lot of buttons. Nearly every single one of them...a little too well.

"You're not a big fan of speed limits, are you?" Santi finally broke the silence after fifteen minutes of oppressive quiet in the front cab of the ambulance.

"I think you meant to say, do you always deal with the heavy traffic of Miami so beautifully, Murphy? Especially since I was late and now require you to take the law into your hands so we can get to our assigned area in time."

"Absolutely. That's exactly what I meant to say." He nodded and grinned, his hand slamming against the dashboard as she took another corner without hitting the brakes. "Practicing for the racetrack?" he threw out, trying to add some more light to her thunderously bad mood. Not that his was all that brilliant.

"You'd better believe it. I've got three races on Saturday and I'm not letting the likes of you hold me back from the winners' circle."

"No joke?" He pushed against the dash, turning in the seat so he could face her, even though her eyes were glued to the road and the last thing he'd be receiving was eye contact.

"I wouldn't joke about something like that." He felt her mood lift.

"What kind of races?"

"Pony car," she answered, as if there weren't any other type of racing. "They might be smaller than the muscle cars but definitely require greater skill at the wheel!" She mimicked a television announcer as she spoke then tacked on a little musical sound-effects riff for added impact, wrapping up with the first smile he'd seen on her lips all day.

"Respect." Santi flick-snapped his fingers and gave a low whistle. So she was a speed junkie. Now, *that* was sexy. He could picture Saoirse in racing gear a little too easily. The image took fireproof underwear to a whole other level of sexy! He swept away a cluster of torrid images and focused on her fingers, snugly tucked around the steering wheel. Three o'clock. Nine o'clock. The girl didn't mess around with one-fingered casual driving. Chances were, she didn't mess around with casual much of anything.

"I'd like to see you in action."

She shot him a quick sidelong glance. "What do you mean by that?"

"Driving. Why? What did you think I meant?"

"Nothing," she answered too quickly, a hit of red streaking along the length of her cheekbones. "Nothing at all."

He turned toward the side window to hide his smile, palm trees and fast-food joints flashing past them at a rate of knots. He seemed to bring out the sandpapery side to Saoirse. How long would it take, he mused, the smile still playing on his lips, to shift the rough to the smooth? Not that he couldn't apply the analogy to himself.

Or know if he had the staying power. Just arriving in Miami—far better by bike than plane—had set off the creeping tendrils of wanderlust. After years abroad he knew his dragon slaying had to happen here, on his home turf. Face up to the responsibilities he'd left behind. But arriving armed with that knowledge wasn't proving to make the task any easier.

A flash of blond caught his eye as Saoirse gave her head a shake, her brain clearly as busy as his was, each of them thinking their way through problems neither of them were ready or willing to share.

All of which suited him just fine.

Working with Murph was shaping up to be a much-needed antidote to the tangle of disasters he was trying to sort out in his personal life.

"Those two chaps..." Saoirse began tentatively, tossing a quick glance in his direction. "The ones standing at the ER desk beside me. Are you related or something?"

The mood in the cab shifted again—the chill factor on his side of the cab increasing by the second.

Santi swallowed the urge to deny fraternity until he'd set things right. He'd come home to fix the fractured bonds, not make them worse. Who knew how dark a white lie could turn if it crept outside the confines of the ambulance?

Her question—innocent enough—was a reminder that he didn't know Saoirse at all and no matter how un-getting-to-know-you their conversation had been up to this point, he wasn't up for this sort of fact-finding mission.

"What makes you say that?"

She made a "duh" sound before putting on a perfect mimicry of a Miami Beach party-girl voice. "I know I'm just a little girlie-wirly, but I have these things called eyes in my head and I used them and then I added up everything I saw and I am beginning to think your parents had more than one child. What's the deal? They seemed all fancy-surgeony. And you obviously know a whole lot more than a paramedic. Why the downgrade?"

"Isn't this a case of the pot calling the kettle black?" Santi shot back. "You're not an 'ordinary' paramedic from what I've seen."

"I used to be a NICU nurse." The information was given reluctantly.

"So do you see yourself as a 'downgraded' specialty nurse?"

Saoirse bit back quickly. "Not in the slightest." *It was just too painful to stay in NICU. All those little babies...*

Her knuckles whitened against the steering wheel as she trotted out her line. "I just felt I could be more hands on when I moved here if I drove an ambulance."

"Ditto."

"But that doesn't explain why you didn't say hi. I mean, they *are* your brothers, aren't they?"

"Qué?"

"You heard me. I saw the look in your eyes. You couldn't get out of there fast enough. What did you do? Steal their lunch money or drop one of them on their heads when they were a baby?"

Santi's left hand shot out instinctively, his fist connecting with the door in a short, sharp punch. *El horno no está para bollos!* "Remind me not to play darts with you, *chica.*"

"Easy, tiger…just wanted to know who I'm stuck with on shift, is all." There was a curl of an apology woven through the shock in her eyes. And more than a little wariness. Santi wouldn't have blamed her if she pulled a wheel-screeching U-turn, headed back to the hospital and requested a new partner. Punching things wasn't his style but she'd aimed, shot and unwittingly scored a bull's-eye. He'd made all of his brothers' lives a whole lot more difficult than they'd needed to be after his parents had been killed, and hauling around the burden of guilt for the last fifteen years had all but buried him.

"Sore subject."

"No kidding," she muttered, slowing the vehicle and pulling into a parking lot across from the beach. She jerked the ambulance to a halt, unclicked her seat belt and shifted around in her seat to look him in the eye. "Right. This is my ambulance—"

"Uh-uh." He shook his head. "I'm the senior one. I was told you were still in training."

"That's just a technicality." Her jaw tightened.

"Not where I come from."

"Where *I* come from—if the so-called senior partner starts acting all crazy we are cruising for Disasterville and I get to call the shots. I don't know about you but I need this job. It's the only thing keeping me sane and you're not helping me keep my cool or my calm. So spill it."

"What?" Not the world's best dodge, but it would buy him a few more seconds.

"Don't prevaricate." She was serious now. "You've got a story and what is it you Americans say? 'Better out than in'? Spill it so we can get your funk out of this cab and focus on work."

"You want my funk?"

She stared at him wide-eyed then burst out laughing. "Yeah." She nodded as the idea settled into place. "Don't ask me why, but lay it on me. I am the funk master."

Santi shook his head. This woman was as mad as a hatter. Good mad. He leaned back against his door, arms folding across his chest as he weighed up the pros and cons of playing along.

"So, what are you saying? You want to do this Vegas-style?"

Crinkles appeared at the top of her nose. "I presume you're not referring to bathing in champagne and luxuriating among satin sheets?"

It hadn't been what he'd been thinking, but now that she mentioned it...

"Whatever floats your boat, *chica*."

Santiago dropped a wink that made more of an impact than Saoirse wished it had. She forced herself to purse her lips and give him an "in your dreams" look.

Then the penny dropped.

She was the one whose mind had slipped straight between the sexy sheets. Her brain played catch-up on the revelation.

"You mean what goes on on the road stays on the road?"

"Exactly." Santi nodded, his full lips curving into a self-satisfied smile. "Glad to see you are keeping your finger on the American pulse."

"That's precisely what I'm trying to do," she said with feeling.

A bit too much feeling for someone who was... er...living in America. She tapped her fingers impatiently on the steering wheel. "Would you hurry up and tell me what has got you all sensitive and girlie—"

"Whoa!" He held up his hands in protest.

"Let's not get carried away here. There's only room for one *princesita* in this cab and it's not—"

Saoirse silenced him with a zip-it yank of her fingers across her mouth. She'd had her princess days and they'd landed her alone and heartbroken. Her fingers crept up to the back of her neck, feeling the short hairs bristle under her touch. It hadn't been that long ago she would have felt her thick hair swish along the small of her back. Her eyes flicked back up to Santi's. By the looks of things he was quite merrily enjoying her discomfort.

Typical overconfident, survival-of-the-fittest *male*! Everything about him, his physique, his confidence, his whole being, exuded *man*. She'd have to develop an immunity to it. And from the effect his eyes alone had on her, now would be a pretty good time to show him his gorgeousness had absolutely no effect on her.

"Enough," she said decisively. "Spill."

"You know, Murphy, you'd be really good at blackmailing people. Or torture. Have you ever considered a career—"

She waved off his attempts to veer off course, making it clear by her gestures that he needed to start talking or get the boot.

"Fine. You got me. They're my brothers."

Saoirse shot a triumphant fist into the air with a whoop and ended up smacking it on the roof of the cab. "Ow! I knew it." She shook her hand

and gave her knuckles a quick covert inspection. "I knew it," she said again, just to make sure he was aware she was still the one in charge here.

"And what are your parents? Doctors or models?"

"Dead."

Saoirse felt her face flame with horror. Talk about open mouth, insert foot. Her parents had been just about the only reason she hadn't flung herself off a jagged cliff edge the day of the wedding-not-wedding. She couldn't imagine not having them at the end of a phone, at the very least. Video links were even better.

"I'm so sorry. I had no idea, Santi."

"Don't worry. You weren't to know." His voice had a heavy dose of robot about it now. She didn't blame him. She couldn't even say her ex-fiancé's name without tearing up, and he was alive and kicking.

The look on Santiago's face said *Don't even think about giving me sympathy,* so she swallowed her pity and ploughed on. If they'd both just endured the worst year ever, they'd finally have something in common.

"Recently?"

"No." He maintained eye contact almost as if he were giving a frontline report to a senior officer that half his men had been killed and the other half had been taken hostage by terrorists.

Her mind reeled back to the intensity with

which he'd fought for the homeless veteran's life yesterday. That hadn't been about saving a stranger's life. It had been about something personal. Something buried away deep in his heart.

She nodded for him to continue.

"My parents were killed twenty years ago at our—at the family bodega. A robbery gone about as wrong as they can when there are guns involved."

He was painting a picture. It was hard to tell whose benefit it was for, but Saoirse clamped her lips tight now that she'd finally got him talking. Not that it made for easy listening. Just hearing the absence of emotion in Santi's voice was chilling.

"I looked after my kid brother, Alejandro, who got snagged by a bullet while my older twin brothers, the ones you saw, went to med school. You were right about the genius part." He marked up a point on the invisible scoreboard hanging between them. "The second I turned eighteen I joined the Marines. Pulled five tours. Now I'm back. Boom. There's your story. Happy now?" His face was anything but.

"Uh…not to be picky or anything, but you sort of left out the part about why you hightailed it out of the ER the second you saw them."

"It's been a while."

From the twitch in his jaw when he clamped his lips tight, Saoirse guessed "a while" would be putting it mildly. She rolled her finger in the "keep it coming" move, surprised she'd already extracted this much information. Too bad she hadn't been this good at "torture" when she'd told her fiancé she couldn't have children and he'd said he was fine with it. How could she have been stupid enough to believe him?

"I've been stationed overseas for a long time now. I didn't think it would be appropriate to do my *holas* after a fifteen-year absence and then... *pum*!" He exploded his fist into an outstretched hand. "*Vamanos*. I'm not sure if you've heard, but my 'boss' is a bit of a whip-cracker," he replied neutrally, although his arched eyebrow dared her to challenge his answer. "Your turn!"

It was pretty clear she'd been given all the information she was going to get. Which, to be fair, was more than she had anticipated. An Irish man would've run for the hills if forced to talk about himself. Vegas-style or otherwise. Which was probably why her ex had chosen the moment before he'd been meant to say "I do" to say "I can't" and had legged it out of the church. It wasn't like she'd given him fair warning she wouldn't be able to have children. It was the exact same amount of time she'd been given. A month to wrap her head around the soul-destroying news and decide to go ahead with the wedding. Too late, she'd realized that sort of news was a deal breaker.

"Earth to Sare-shee."

Why couldn't anyone get her name right? *Sear-shuh, Sear-shuh, Sear-shuh!*

She shot him a glare and grabbed the radio mic that was yabbering away for a callback.

"It's *Murphy*," she growled at him, before picking up. "This is Ambulance 23 at Mar Vista, ready to respond."

They listened to the static-filled voice in silence. "Vehicle 23, we have a three-month-old infant presenting with fever and difficulty breathing." The address came out in a clear, staccato, lightly accented voice.

"Got it." She signed out, giving a sober-faced Santi a quick nod as she turned the key in the ignition and he flicked on the sirens.

Sharing time would have to wait.

CHAPTER FOUR

"Look, there she is." Santi pointed toward the end of the block where a woman was running down the lawn with a swaddled child in her arms.

Saoirse pulled the vehicle alongside the frantic mother seconds later.

"You do immediate attending, I'll get the gear ready," she commanded, before flying out of the cab to open up the back.

"I thought you were the one in training. All experience is good experience."

"Not today I'm not." There was an edge to her voice, different from the professional terseness he'd seen the day before. There was definitely a story there. He yanked his stethoscope from around his neck and jumped out of the vehicle. Another time, another place.

"My baby's not breathing! Please help my little boy!" The mother held the child in her outstretched arms toward Santi. While very pale, the baby boy had streaks of color in his cheeks, so he was clearly getting some oxygen, but even with Saoirse's high-octane slamming of doors and the growing chatter of onlookers he could hear a rattle in the child's quick, painful-sounding breaths.

"What's his name?"

"Carlos—same as his *papi*. I'm Maria-Rose."

"That's a good, strong name for a boy." Santiago took the child in his arms. Calming the parent was often half the trick in cases like this. "Has Carlos produced any phlegm, Maria-Rose?" he asked, steering the mother toward the ambulance and unwrapping the blanket. Children weren't his forte, though he'd tended to his fair share of locals on his tours. The humanitarian side of being in the military had always appealed to him far more than treating victims of actual combat. He stopped the memories in midflow, quickly pulling back the child's blanket and sleep suit. He hoped when he got the child fully unclothed he wouldn't see a rash. The little boy's cheek was hot to the touch and he wasn't crying at all.

She shook her head. "He has been very lethargic, whining more than crying through the night. And then there's that blue tinge to his tongue. Can you see it?"

He gently opened the boy's mouth with his fingers and saw there was a blue tinge not only to his tongue but on the inside of his lips as well.

"We'd better get your son some oxygen." He quickly ran through the child's medical history with Maria-Rose, immunizations, no problems with the birth to speak of, and onset of symptoms.

"Just the past day or so that I've noticed." She wrung her hands nervously, as if she'd given the wrong answer. Timing was critical with small children. She'd been wise to call for emergency services.

"Only twenty-four hours? Okay. Any trips since he's been born?" he asked, pressing his stethoscope to the child's chest only to hear the thick rattle that said one thing: pneumonia.

The mother shook her head.

"Good. What about you? Did you travel at all while you were pregnant?" From what he'd heard, there were lots of problems with women unknowingly affected by the Zika virus. He ran his hand across the child's scalp—it felt normal size—so nothing to obviously suggest he, too, was a victim of the mosquito-borne affliction.

"Are you kidding?" She threw up her hands. "We've been saving all our money to go to Carlos and his education."

The same as his parents had done. Sacrificed everything so their children could have it all. The closest they'd come to "returning" to their homeland of Heliconia had been Vizcaya on Biscayne Bay. The tropical gardens had always sent his mother into raptures of homesickness.

The weight of the child in his arms realigned his focus.

"Good. Any problems feeding?"

"In here, Santi." Saoirse waved him to the back of the ambo, climbing up the steps as he approached.

"What do you need?"

Santi's brain shot from information gathering to action mode. "High-flow oxygen, amoxicillin—"

"Did you check for allergies?" Saoirse's tone was sharp but not accusatory. Safety first and all that.

"Yes. No allergies that the mother is aware of." He took the oxygen tube she offered and gently taped it in place on the little boy's face. "Can you inject the antibiotics into the saline solution please? Until we get cultures at the hospital we won't know exactly what we're dealing with but I'm pretty sure it's pneumonia."

"Do you see that?" Saoirse's voice was low.

Santi narrowed his eyes and nodded after a moment. A rash. "Do you have any slides? It could be nothing, but it could just as easily be invasive pneumococcal."

"Septicemia?" She handed him a slide, nodding at his diagnosis.

"Maybe, or Zika—but I don't think the Zika

rash manifests like this. Have you seen any cases?" Santi pressed the clear slide against the boy's skin, nodding as Saoirse said she'd heard about it but had never seen a case. "It blanches. That's a good thing."

"Doesn't mean there isn't septicemia," she whispered, aware the boy's mother was straining to hear everything they said.

"True." He nodded. "Let's get an IV into this little guy and hit the road."

"Yup. I'd just like to test his fontanelle before we head off."

Santi slipped in the IV, aware of how crucial fluids were for a sick child, all the while ratcheting up a few more respect points for Saoirse. Her experience as a NICU nurse clearly put her miles ahead of your average trainee paramedic. Most wouldn't know their way around pediatric lingo with the comfort level she was displaying. Or exhibit unerring competency in the crucial tests as she was.

Someone, he thought as he watched her finish the examination of the baby's head while he secured the IV line, has a bit of a history.

"What do you feel?" Santi asked after a moment's silence.

"It's not tense. No swelling. Hopefully, it's not meningitis." Saoirse pressed herself up from the bench, hoping her face bore nothing more than a picture of professional efficiency. "Right, Maria-Rose. Do you want to jump in and we'll get your little man to Seaside Hospital for some tests, okay?"

As she slammed the doors shut, she saw Santi as the rest of the world might see him. Gorgeous, yes. But there was something deeper than that. A skilled paramedic, body taut with focus, driven to do the best he could for the small child laid out on the gurney.

He *cared*.

Santi was in this all the way, no showboating. And that was something she could relate to. What you saw was what you got. For the most part, anyway.

She pulled open the driver's door and flicked on the sirens with a grin. Maybe her new partner wouldn't be so bad after all.

"Here you are, Murph. One I-survived-a-week-with-Santi Café Cubano."

Saoirse eyed the small cup warily. "This isn't going to keep me up all night, is it?"

Santi's lips shifted into a mischievous grin with a quick lift of his dark eyebrows. "*Por qué?* Does Mamacita Murphy have a hot date tonight?"

"Quit doing that!"

"What?"

"That whole…" she opened her hand and

"washed" it around his face "...Latin Lothario thingy."

"You don't like my sexy, sexy talk?" He cranked it up another few notches.

Yes.

"Doesn't work on me."

Liar, liar pants on fire.

She avoided catching his eye just to be safe.

"But it has on someone else..." Santi poked her in the arm. "Who's the lucky guy tonight, Murph?"

Why was he so interested in who she was dating anyhow? Wasn't quizzing her all day on her emergency medicine knowledge enough Q & A?

She smirked in lieu of swooning, then pursed her lips together and blew a raspberry. "That's me. A regular ol' dating machine."

She continued to give her tiny cup of coffee the evil eye. There had been so much change in her life over the last year. Becoming single. Realizing she was never going to have children. Hopping on a plane with a student visa instead of the fiancée visa, which had expired...about six months ago now. *Urgh!*

The switch from hot, milky tea to coffee had been hard enough. She'd have to call her mum and have her send some proper tea bags over.

A chill of realization hit her. Even if the tea arrived in a week, she would be gone in a couple of months. April Fools' Day. The irony! Deported back to Ireland unless, by some divine intervention, she found a man bonkers enough to marry her.

"It's not going to bite you."

"What is it again?" She held the small cup up at eye level then gave it a dubious sniff.

"A Café Cubano. It's the closest thing to heaven after a hard day and, *orale*—you were on it today, *mija!*" Santi did that whizzy snap thing with his fingers again and crowed. She nodded, feigning accepting a loud roar of applause from a stadium full of fans. *As if.*

"Teamwork, Valentino. It all boils down to teamwork."

And she meant it. They'd only had a week together in the ambulance but already they had a partner shorthand going on that made working together a genuine pleasure. Even if she sometimes had to squint at him and turn his gorgeousness into a blur of caramel features. Santiago Valentino would be far too easy to fall for. And love? That little nugget of complications was well and truly off the table.

"Here." He handed her an open bottle of water. "Take a swig of this to cleanse your palate and then drink the *cafecito*."

"My, my," Saoirse play-crooned, happy to yank her thoughts away from the thunderstorm brewing in her head. "Isn't someone Mr. *Exotico*?"

"That's rich, coming from the leprechaunette of Miami Beach."

"Whatever." Saorise leaned back against the slatted bench and narrowed her eyes. Santi's good looks screamed exotic, but his accent, when he spoke English, was as American as they came. When he spoke Spanish with non-English-speaking patients and turned on the Latino thing? Mmm-hmm... Hard to shake off just how sexy he was. That beautifully sensual mouth, inky-black hair and a body that would've been more than worth watching if he was dancing *la vida loca*.

Good thing they were just colleagues.

She looked at him again then looked away.

Pah-ha-ha! Try telling that to the judge.

Tentatively, she stepped back into the muddy waters of family history, "Your parents were from...?"

"Heliconia. It's a little island nation out..." He pointed away from the hospital toward the sea, his sentence tapering off as his hand fell back into his lap.

"And they brought you over with them when you were little?" Saoirse pressed gently.

"Before we were born," he answered, the life all but draining from his eyes.

"You and your brothers?" She stated the obvious, already preparing her "Oops, I shouldn't have said that" face, only to receive a quick no-eye-contact nod in return before he downed his coffee in one swift go. He hadn't said a word about them the entire week and it looked like that would be the status quo.

"Right!" He flicked the paper cup into the garbage can with an ease that told her this wasn't his first Café Cubana rodeo. "I think we've heard enough about me to last a lifetime. Why don't we go into the hospital, see if we can rustle up a transfer or something? Maybe over to Buena Vista. The private hospitals always have much better cantinas."

"Sounds good to me." Saoirse knew when to stop digging. She had her own full-to-bursting cupboard of secrets so there was no point in poking around someone else's. She slurped down her coffee in the same quick style as Santi, only to have her body reel from the effects. "For the love of Peter, Paul and Mary!"

Santi wasn't the only strong, dark thing in town.

"What are you trying to do to me?" She glared at him while stuffing the paper cup into the garbage can. "Put hairs on my chest or something?"

Santi threw back his head and laughed. A rich, warm laugh that never failed to make her smile. Unexpectedly he reached out and ran a finger along her jawline, tipping her chin up to meet his gaze.

"*Dulzera*, believe me..." Despite the bright

midday sunshine, Santi's voice went all tropical-nights sultry on her, sending little shivers down her spine as their eyes connected. "There isn't a single thing I would change about you."

His words set her insides jigging about as if she'd just won the lottery. The last thing she'd felt since her fiancé had left her at the altar had been feminine, but the surge of I-am-woman Santi's touch unleashed? Far too easy to let rip and roar.

And then he winked, the warm light burning bright in his eyes, giving Saoirse another unexpected shot of pleasure. Unwitting or not, she liked being the one who'd turned that frown of his into a smile. It was one worth waiting for. If she didn't watch it… She pulled back and broke eye contact, tugging her fingers through the short pixie cut she was still getting used to as she did…

She'd just have to watch it.

"C'mon, slowpoke. Let's go get that transfer."

"High five!"

"What for?" Saoirse asked, pulling a fresh sheet onto the gurney for the next crew.

"One amazing nightclubber save—" Santi counted them off on his fingers "—even though you had to go down into the drain ditch and you stink to high heaven." He pinched his nose then returned to his counting. "Two beach rescues, a broken arm splinted expertly by myself, of course, three hospital transfers and a head wound from a machete beautifully sutured by your good self. That's what I call a good day with ALSA!"

Santi gave the inside of the ambulance door a final squirt of disinfectant and swipe of a blue paper towel before standing back to admire their handiwork.

"Who's Alsa?" Saoirse climbed out of the back of the cab, having finished her restock, and joined him in the ambulance appreciation stance. Crossed arms, legs slightly apart, hips pushed slightly forward to allow for a bit of backward-leaning and head-nodding.

"Number 23, ding-a-ling! Haven't you learned anything from your wise mentor? Advanced Life Support Ambulance." He gave her a joshing elbow in the ribs. "That's what they're called, Little Miss Shamrock."

"Ah, stick a four-leaf clover in it, would you? Joe was old school—he used all his big-boy words. No ALSA this or EMT that," she gibed, obviously covering for the fact she'd been driving Ambulance 23 for two and a half months now and didn't know the acronym. She quickly pointed a wagging index finger at him. "And the four-leaf clover thing, by the way, is not something all Irish people say. It's a special saying for the likes of lippy Latinos who look a lot like you."

* * *

Saoirse swatted his arm kid-sister-style, her hand bouncing off a biceps Santi managed to flex just in the nick of time.

He grinned as she feigned breaking her hand. So she made him want to show off a little. So what? Saoirse had never shown a flicker of interest in him and it kept things…workable.

"There are so many acronyms to learn in this fair nation of yours. I'll never get my head round them. Not that—" She cut herself short, the quick flick of her eyes making it clear Santi was the last person she was going to use as a confessor.

"Not that you call them the same thing in Ireland?" He dodged the conversational bullet for her.

"Beats me." She widened her bright blue eyes. "I just called them ambulances. I wasn't on them at ho—in Ireland," she corrected herself.

Interesting. Times two.

"I'm guessing you didn't learn to be such a hotshot paramedic overnight." A compliment never hurt when extracting information. "Did you say it was Pediatrics you were in?"

He knew damn well it wasn't, but she'd heard his story…time for a bit of quid pro quo and all that.

"NICU," she bit out, grabbing the roll of paper towel from him, before executing a brisk about-face and marching off to the supplies room.

Santi watched her trim, jumpsuit-clad figure stomp off, heard a couple of locker doors slam once she'd disappeared around the corner and, if he wasn't mistaken, some grouchy muttering.

It appeared he wasn't the only one with sore spots. Then again, who didn't hit their thirties without a bit of baggage? He'd wrestled her age out of her earlier in the day when she'd complained about having to show ID every time she wanted a drink. A baby-faced thirty to his more "seasoned" thirty-three.

He huffed out a sigh. The last few years had most definitely added to the steamer trunks of issues he'd been filing away since the ripe age of thirteen. Not as early as some, but losing your parents and nearly losing one of your brothers when all the kids around you were worried about acne and homework was tough.

Working extensively in war zones gave stark reminders that bad things happened everywhere. He understood now that his family hadn't been singled out. They hadn't been targeted for having too much, being too happy or living the American dream. They had just been the hapless victims of a gang initiation meant to be carried out in a different bodega. So-called "friendly fire." It had been sheer devastation at the time. Still was on some days. But it could have happened to anyone.

Even so, he didn't like seeing Saoirse the sad

side of heated up. She suited firecracker to a T...
but he felt certain something in her was more be-
reaved than belligerent.

"Hey," he called out when she reappeared.
"You up for a margarita at Ron's?"

She considered him for a moment, visibly trying to detect if there was an agenda attached to
the invitation, her lips curling in and out of her
mouth in a move he was fairly certain wasn't designed to turn him on, but did. He shifted. Maybe
the whole work buddies just having a drink thing
was a bit precipitous.

"Yeah. Why not?" she answered, just as he
was about to withdraw the invitation. "I just need
to pop in and see Amanda for a minute." She
tipped her head toward the main hospital building, hands gingerly holding her backpack as if
it were made of glass.

"Sure." He easily matched the quick pace she
was setting, having the advantage of longer legs.
"I'll come with you and we can shoot off from
there. You cool with riding on the back of a bike?
I have a spare helmet."

"The old-fashioned number?" A glint of delight lit up her features. "Only if you promise to
take the long way round."

He nodded with a happy smile. A lot of Miami
girls wouldn't dare jump on for fear of messing
up their hair.

"For you, *mija*? That is an easy enough promise to make." He held the palm of his hand out for a down-low high-five and when she met it his fingers folded around hers. And for just a few seconds—if someone had been looking—they would have seemed like an ordinary couple holding hands. What he wouldn't give for a slice of ordinary right now. Or normal, whatever that was. Something that didn't feel like suffocating in the place he should've felt most at home.

He glanced to his right.

Maybe this was just what he'd needed when he'd decided to leave the military and face his past. Even if just for a few micromoments, when he was holding hands with Saoirse, he felt…free. Unencumbered by the past that made coming home so painful. An Everest of issues. That was what he was facing. And if Saoirse's presence in his life was that all-important oxygen tank? He could start to breathe just that little bit more easily.

Saoirse tugged her hand out of Santi's as nonchalantly as a girl who was having a panic attack could.

As long as conversations were about medicine, motorbikes or her upcoming track sessions she was cool. But being touched by Santiago and feeling amazing when it happened? She couldn't go there.

Pals, buddies, workmates? *Good.*

Tingly, giggly, girlie feelings? *Bad.*

Muy bad, as Santi would say. *Not that she'd started stealing his go-to phrases or anything.*

Maybe just accepting the fact her visa was going to run out soon would be the best option. It might not be pretty, but she didn't have to live a double life back in Ireland. Everyone knew she wasn't marrying Tom or going to have children—so no awkward conversations there. Virtually the entire village she'd grown up in had borne witness to her standing on her lonesome at the altar...just a few minutes after they'd all gasped with pleasure when she'd appeared at the doorway of the church in all her bridal glory. So...if she buckled and went back, she could comfortably look forward to a lifetime of people talking behind their hands and a wealth of pitying looks being shot her way as she pootled toward an eternity of spinsterhood.

Gah!

Alternatively...

There were nunneries liberally dappled across Ireland, all of them as keen as anything for nurses to show up and care for their aging populations... She scrunched her eyes shut for a second, trying to picture herself in a wimple.

Not too bad.

"What was that?" Santi was looking at her curiously.

Uh-oh. Out-loud voice strikes again.

"I was just agreeing. Belatedly. About the day. Not bad."

Excellent cover, you ol' smooth operator, you! She shot through the sliding glass doors of the ER, grateful for the blast of air-con on her flushed skin. "You can just stay here while I go find—"

"Ah! There you are." Amanda was by her side and reaching for her backpack before Saoirse had a chance to register the fact her friend was all sun-dressed up, bikini strings snaking around from the back of her neck. "It's hot out. Want to come for a swim before James has a look at this?"

"Ah, well…"

Amanda was quicker than Saoirse at picking up the situation. "Sorry, my bad. James said he wanted a swim *à deux* today. The joys of married life!" She wriggled her wedding band hand in front of the pair of them then tipped her index finger down toward Saoirse's backpack. "This got everything in it?"

"Yes." Saoirse nodded, suddenly very aware her entire life was in the green backpack and that Santiago was bearing witness to the handover. Her fingers tightened around the top of it as if all of her lacy panties were going to come flying out if her grip wasn't secure enough.

Santi laughed. "Good grief, Murphy. You look like you're about to hand over state secrets."

Saoirse tried to wipe the panic-stricken expression off her face as Amanda jumped in, her face wreathed in smiles. "Close enough, Santiago! The truth is, we need someone to marry our little Irish Rose here or else she's going to get shipped back outta Dodge in a few short months. As you've probably figured out, she's here on a student trainee visa and once the course is up…?"

She made a get-outta-Dodge signal with her thumb. "Back to Ireland. My husband is an immigration lawyer. He's going to check over all of her paperwork to make sure there isn't something else we can do, maybe extend the student thing, but our girl's a bit too bright for her own good and the clock is ticking. Since the *last thing* in the world she can do is go back to Ireland, we've got to find her a path to a green card. And fast. Like…" she paused for effect "…a quickie marriage, for example."

"Are you out of your *mind*?" Saoirse's jaw hung open in disbelief. A puff of air-con could've knocked her over.

"This Murphy?" Santi asked, finger pointing at Saoirse, eyes trained on Amanda, who had mysteriously become the source of all wisdom. "What's she done that she can't go home? Committed a felony or something?"

"No. But her ex-fiancé near enough did."

Saoirse's eyes swung from one face to the

other, each chatting about the darkest moment in her life as if it were a daytime soap.

"What did he do?" He gave Saoirse's shoulder a little pat, the kindly sort a person would give to a toddler whose ice cream had just plopped onto a hot sidewalk after they'd had their first satisfying lick of salted caramel. Or something like that.

She gave him a hooded look and muttered, "I don't really think that's any of your business." Not that she was being offered even the slightest bit of participation in this conversation.

"He abandoned our beautiful, blushing bride here. *At the altar,*" Amanda added with award-winning dramatics.

"Oh, for the love of—"

"Uh-uh, honey. Not done yet." Amanda gave her the conciliatory pat on the shoulder this time. "In my book? What he did to Murph is totally a jail-able offense, but…" She made a little lock-up-and-throw-away-the-key gesture in front of her smiling lips. "That's not my business to tell."

"I repeat, have you gone absolutely stark raving *mad*?" Saoirse's cheeks were flaming hot. This was feeling every bit as mortifying as the moment her ex had looked at her when given his "I do" cue, looked at the congregation, the priest, back to her…and had then legged it straight out of the church as if she'd been on the verge of giving him the plague.

It wasn't as if she'd turned green and sprouted a beard. She simply couldn't give him children.

He'd said it wasn't a deal breaker when they'd both been blindsided by the news a month earlier. A big enough deal to throw her to the gossip wolves of Kincarney village was more like it.

She swallowed. Hard. She was not—no way, no how—*not* going to cry in front of Santi.

"How long have you got?" Santiago asked, his attention now fully on her.

"Why? What's it got to do with you?" Saoirse only just stopped herself from physically recoiling at his let's-get-serious expression.

"Well, I was going to offer…" He shrugged then turned to Amanda. "But seeing as the idea seems utterly repugnant to Murphy here—"

What?

"I guess I won't bother."

Wait a minute! Her mind fuzzed with too much to process.

What?

A little *no-no-no* whimper came out of her before she could stop it. Sure, she wanted to stay in Miami more than anything, but not with… with…*Mr. Perfect*!

"Oh, don't listen to Murphy. We accept!" Amanda jumped in, charming as a stewardess getting everyone to buckle up on a bumpy flight. "She's a bit…" Amanda turned, crooking her arms through Santi's and her own as she steered them all out into the early evening warmth and chose her words carefully. "Murphy's a bit… *shy*…of relationships right now."

"Suits me," Santi riposted, seemingly unaffected by the scowl growing on Saoirse's face. "I have no plans to get married myself so I might as well earn some brownie points with the best partner I've ever had on an ambulance."

"I'm the *only* partner you've ever had on an ambulance," Saoirse shot back, wondering how he could be so…*cavalier* about all of this.

Santiago Valentino was a still-waters-running-deep kind of guy. That was easy enough to divine amid his wisecracking, lighthearted approach to things. Something didn't feel right about this. And she wasn't going to be hoodwinked into agreeing to it. Not for one second.

Blanking her completely, Amanda continued, "And for the record, because I don't want to see my dear friend Sohr-shuh—"

"It's *Murphy*!"

"As I was saying before I was so rudely interrupted, I won't have my dear friend *Sear-shuh* hurt again. This has to be strictly business. So, Santiago…why exactly do you think a quickie marriage with no emotional ties whatsoever is for you?" Amanda was clearly relishing the role of Chief Marital Prospects Interviewer.

Saoirse was almost relieved to see the smile disappear from Santi's lips. Finally! A bit of reality was sinking in. Sure, she needed a visa, but not with someone so...so fall-in-love-with-able. If she'd thought her first almost marriage had been doomed, this one had lightning strikes and heavy clouds gathering around it from the get-go.

"Let's just say..." Santi began carefully, then abruptly turned his considered expression back to nonchalant. "Like I said, it's always good to earn some brownie points with the boss lady."

She'd seen that shift in Santiago before. The one where he was all frowny and serious one minute and then transformed into Santi the Fun-Loving Clown the next.

It was the fake-it-till-you-believe-it-yourself sort of mask she'd worn often enough to spot another's a mile off.

Agreeing to this harebrained scheme was big. Of the megatropolis variety of big.

"Right." Saoirse jabbed a finger in his chest. "You. Me. Mad Ron's. *Now.*"

"The little lady has spoken!" Amanda trilled, waving them off as if they were heading to their honeymoon.

"Where's your motorcycle?" Saoirse glowered.

"Just over there, across from the ambulance bay."

"Good. Can there just...?" She waved her hand between them, doing her best to swallow down the swell of nausea threatening to bloom. "Just no talking on the way there."

* * *

"Here, put this on." Santi shrugged off his leather jacket and held it out for Saoirse to put on. He couldn't tell how much responsibility he bore for the murderous expression working its way malevolently across her features.

"Uh-uh. You keep it. I don't need your help. Leather or otherwise."

A fair bit, then.

"You've got goose bumps all over your arms."

"They're goose *pimples* where I come from," she retorted.

"Well, unless you want to go back to where you come from, I suggest you put this on and we go talk about your friend's proposal. Or—more accurately—*my* proposal."

Okay. That was a sentence he'd never thought he'd hear himself say.

He gave the coat a pointed shake directly in Saoirse's eye line, lifting a finger from the black leather to make the spinning-around gesture so he could slip it on her. Something a husband would do.

Dios.

He was sliding into the fictional husband slippers a bit too easily. Cinderella, on the other hand, wasn't interested in increasing her shoe count.

The lines between real and fake were going to be blurry. In the eyes of the world? He'd be a real husband for a real woman. A woman glaring at him for acting chivalrous.

Mars and Venus popped into mind. *Saoirse on a half shell...*

"I'm not helpless, you know." His unbetrothed yanked the coat out of his hands and stuffed her arms into the sleeves.

"So you keep saying."

Saoirse's temper at the prospect of marrying him was rapidly unearthing something deep inside him. Something organically at odds with what he knew to be true.

He wasn't reliable.

He wasn't someone who was there when it counted.

And yet with each passing moment he wanted to do this.

A chance to prove he had staying power that wasn't entirely selfish? Hell, yeah!

He felt his shoulders sink...just a fraction.

Force himself to prove he had staying power was more like it.

The veneer of elation he'd felt at volunteering suffered a fault line.

Making a commitment like this would be...a commitment. One he couldn't break.

He watched as Saoirse shrugged into the oversize leather jacket, becoming aware, as he did, how good it made him feel to—in just this little gesture of keeping her safe and warm—be looking after her.

¡Dale! It would feel good to be believed in again.

Field medics were under such pressure to do the best they could by the men they fought alongside, and the more he'd lost… It was tough to keep the whole thing at arm's length. There were only so many jokes a man could pull when he's living in hell every day.

Basta.

It was why he was here. Why he'd come back after the stream of coffins he'd been forced to send home had become too much.

He'd learned early on how quickly a life could just…disappear.

Not more than a few feet away from him, his own mother's life had been snuffed out right in front of his thirteen-year-old eyes. Life was short and he'd be damned if he was going to his own grave without his brothers knowing the millstone of remorse he'd dragged around the globe. He'd become good at pretending it wasn't eating him alive. Too good.

Marrying Saoirse would cement him to the ground long enough to make good with his brothers and—Lord willing—give his bride a bit more sunshine in those glowering eyes of hers.

He reached out to tug up the zip on the jacket, only to have his hands slapped away.

"I've got it!"

"Fine." He unhooked the spare helmet from his bike seat. "Here." He put the helmet on her head, elbowing away her hands when she tried to attach the straps herself. "*I* always check the straps." He snapped the clasps together, eyes glued to hers, before giving the straps a quick tug to make sure they were secure. The more she scowled, the more he could feel his lips peeling into a broad grin. This marriage arrangement didn't have to be all work and no play.

"Are we ready yet?" Saoirse tapped her foot impatiently.

"Not just yet." He considered her for a moment.

Leisurely.

Tropical blue eyes crackling with frustration. Body taut with tension, appearing almost fragile in the oversize bulk of his leather jacket. Little wisps of blonde hair softening the edges of the black half helmet. Instinct overrode intellect as he cupped her chin in his hand and dropped a soft peck on her lips.

Just as he'd thought. Salty *and* sweet.

"Now you're ready," he told her, lips brushing against hers as he spoke.

Without waiting to gauge her response, he swung a leg over his bike and revved it up, certain the beefy roar of the engine was drowning out a colorful response.

* * *

There might have been no talking, but Saoirse's body language was speaking louder than any voice could have as Santi casually wove along the seafront on the way to Mad Ron's Cantina. He grinned when he felt Saoirse's fingers hook onto his belt buckle in an attempt not to wrap her arms around his waist. The first corner he hit, he took the bike at a low angle, hoping instinct would take over and she'd wrap her arms around his waist.

Nope.

She threw her hands behind her and was holding onto the rack he strapped his gear to.

Pity.

This was, hands down, the strangest wooing he'd ever done.

Not that he'd had a lot of active duty in the Romeo department. A life in the military made hooking up relatively easy and shipping out even easier. No promises. No hard feelings.

He resisted reaching back to give Saoirse's leg a reassuring rub, revving the bike up a gear instead. She'd said she liked fast things.

Or was it that she liked things fast? This... whatever it was with Saoirse was invading his barred-to-all-visitors emotional zone at high speed. Not that he was planning on giving the woman a life of wedded bliss, it was just a good deed thing, but...

He swore under his breath. *It was a chance, wasn't it?* A chance to prove to someone he could be there when it counted.

Santi took the long route as per Saoirse's earlier request, fairly certain, given the change of events, she would've preferred the express train to a margarita.

With the wind on his face, the remains of the sun on his arms and a smile on his lips, the idea of marrying Saoirse continued to grow on him. Big time. It was win-win all around. Particularly if they could get back to the playful banter they shared at work.

And no more lonely nights. It would be nice to have someone to joke with over fish tacos at dinner... Big brother, little sister with—okay—a bit of frisson thrown in. But he could check his libido at the altar.

She wanted to stay and couldn't. He *needed* to stay and prove to himself he could do right by someone. Preferably his brothers, but he might as well start on more neutral territory. Neutral-ish, anyhow.

Saoirse's chin rammed into Santi's back when he hit the brakes a bit too quickly at a stop sign... *accidentally on purpose.* She jabbed him in the ribs in retaliation.

He smiled.

At least they had the bickering couple thing down to a fine art.

CHAPTER FIVE

"I REPEAT, YOU are an angel."

"Sí, mija," the forty-something bartender replied drily. "That's my name."

"But you actually *do* nice things, too," Saoirse added, before ducking underneath the bar's closable in-and-out flap to get to Ángel's side. "Like letting innocent young ladies such as myself hide behind the bar until they can sneak out the back." She tacked on an eyelashes flutter for good measure.

"Who's sneaking where?" Santi sidled up to the bar, visibly enjoying the fact he'd caught his "fiancée" in midescape. He put on his caveman voice. "C'mon over here, woman. We've got a wedding to plan!"

Was it wrong that Saoirse found the combo of a commanding voice and an überfit Marine body demanding her presence *sexy*?

Yes! And a thousand times *yes*, on so many levels, yes, yes, yes.

Even though… She pursed her lips as she eyed

Santi from the safety of the other side of the bar. How easy would it be to order a cave-girl outfit?

"You're getting married?" Ángel's eyes were wide with disbelief. And not the good kind. He was looking at Santi as if he'd just made the worst decision in the universe.

"Hey!" Saoirse demanded. "What's so revolting about someone wanting to marry me?"

"Ah! So you *do* want to marry me now." Santi gave her a satisfied smirk.

"Both of you are crazy." Ángel shook his head and started muttering in Spanish. "*Muy loco. Here.*" He quickly poured out two shots of tequila and pushed them across the counter. "You take these. Go have a talk in the garden about babies and mortgages and diapers and phone calls right when you're in the middle of dominoes with the guys and the divorce you never saw coming and visiting your kids when, and only when, their *mami* deems you worthy, and *then* you tell me if you're still on." He fixed both of them with a disappointed smile before shooing Saoirse out from behind the bar while twirling his index finger by his head. *"Loco. Totalmente!"*

The pair of them walked toward the patio in silence, Santi holding their shots and Saoirse using both hands to transport her supersize margarita, wondering, just for a moment, how gauche it would be if she were to take a sweet and sour slug of it right now. Her mind was whirling with its own cocktail of horror, panic and, surprisingly, sadness at Ángel's words. Santi hadn't even begun the ridiculous fake-marriage adventure and already it was being kiboshed with a gritty dose of embittered ex-husband? If he wouldn't marry her for pretend, who would ever marry her for real?

When they sat down, they solemnly clinked glasses and threw back the tangy tequila, letting it shudder down their spines as it took effect.

Santi gave Saoirse the most sober look she thought she'd ever seen him wear.

"Well," he began somberly, "I guess we know who's not up for being best man."

Laughter didn't even begin to cover Saoirse's response to the tension-cutting comment. It was an all-body-encompassing giggle, snort, companionable watering-eyes laugh-until-the-tears-started-falling-out response.

When she finally had the wherewithal to wipe her eyes and stop laughing she met Santi's inquisitive gaze and realized they were at a crossroads.

"All right, Murph, it's time to get real." Santi took a long draft of ice water as if it were some sort of strongman tonic. *Like Mr. Muscles needed it.* "Are we going to do this thing?"

"Look…um…" Saoirse opted to draw designs

in the water rings her margarita had left on the table in lieu of looking at Santi. "Don't you even want to know the story?"

Santi shrugged. "I trust you, but if it would make you feel better…"

"Ha! I know you, you sly old dog. Very clever. Trying to wheedle the truth out of me by pretending not to care." It was a weak dodge but, *wow,* did she hate talking about herself. Even if she'd been the one to offer.

"Of course I care—but if you don't want to tell me, you don't have to. That's all I'm saying." And he looked like he meant it. Saoirse felt her heart swell with gratitude. And a little bit of something else she thought she'd better shove right back wherever it had come from.

"I feel like I owe it to you." That much was true. If he was going to just casually enter into a state of wedded bliss with her, he might as well know why.

"Fair enough."

Santi signaled to the waitress to bring them a menu before refocusing on Saoirse, who was giving him her best you're-joking-with-me-aren't-you face.

"What?" he protested. "If we're going to be here awhile, I might as well fortify myself. Have you tried the *carnitas*? Ron makes them." He kissed his fingertips in appreciation. *"Muy delicioso."*

"Want them at the wedding reception?" Saoirse joked.

"Qué?" This time the glint of humor was missing in his eyes. "You want the whole white wedding thing after…after…?"

"What? You mean after getting utterly humiliated in front of everyone I'd ever met in my entire life because my fiancé couldn't take it that it turned out I can't have children?"

There was probably a less embittered way to describe the moment when all of her marital dreams had gone up in smoke, but right now she couldn't think of one.

The waitress appeared as Santi's jaw was still dropping. Saoirse tersely ordered two plates of *carnitas* and a bucket of tortilla chips. Extra-salty. She waved her hand before the waitress had turned away and doubled the order. She loved those things and if Santi was going to bail on her now, she might as well eat her body weight in tortillas before heading back to Ireland. It wouldn't matter if she was the size of a whale because nuns' habits were extra accommodating and from the looks of things a life of solitary confinement behind a thick stone wall was the only thing on offer.

Santi was looking absolutely mortified and she had half a mind to get up and leave. But when she'd come so far in so few months only to give up at the final—albeit very, very monumentally tall—hurdle? No way.

"You're all right, Santi. Don't you worry. I don't want the whole white wedding with lollipop-colored bridesmaids, if that's what's keeping you so slack-jawed," Saoirse said.

"No," he responded quickly. "I just can't believe a man who truly loved a woman would walk out on her like that. For such a ridiculous reason."

"I guess he wanted children a whole lot more than he wanted me," she said without self-pity "I never realized how much I wanted them until I found out I couldn't. Come to think of it, if you want children of your own, this whole thing would be really stupid for you."

"Why?"

"Uh—the age thing?"

"I'll be virile in my nineties, *chica*," Santi countered with a sly fox grin.

"You wish. C'mon. It's important. Have you thought about having children?"

"I've never really thought about it."

It was a semitruthful response. Of course he'd love children. One day. But the checklist of things he needed to set right was a long one. And until he felt all the i's had been dotted and t's crossed? It was for the best he wasn't adding babies into the mix. Babies and the women who had them generally wanted a real wedding. A real *marriage*. Like his parents had shared. He knew he'd probably idealized the memories a bit by now but…

He swore silently. Those days were gone. Artifice was a good starting point for him.

Saoirse propped her chin in her cupped hand and stared at him. Hard. "And you are absolutely sure it doesn't bother you that if we do this thing, you'll be off the proverbial market for the next couple of years while I wait to get my green card?"

A lot of things bothered him. Spending time with Saoirse wasn't one of them.

"Why do you want to live here so badly?" It was easier to bounce questions off her than answer her probing questions.

"Because it's the total opposite of everything I know," she answered, her face lighting up as if she'd found her true place in the world. "I know I haven't been in Miami for long, but I feel like I *belong* here." She smiled as the waitress slipped a basket of warm tortilla chips onto the table. After munching through a handful, she leaned forward, elbows perched on the picnic table, body alive with whatever it was she was formulating in that overactive brain of hers.

Whoever won her heart in the end, he realized, would be winning pure gold. Would he really be able to do this and not get attached? Not... wonder?

He tuned in to what she was saying, realizing that simply staring at her lips was very likely a failure in the fiancé department.

"Back home, everyone knew everything about me so making decisions, doing anything at all—my job, my hair, my clothes—and choices weren't an option. It was as though my life had already been written in stone, you know?"

Santi nodded his head, but he didn't. Until his parents had been killed everything had been about choices, opportunities. His parents had moved their world straight into the heart of the oyster that was meant to hold all the pearls. It had been up to him and his brothers to reach out and grab the right one. And when their lives had been so brutally ended?

Everything he'd thought a childhood should have been had been swept under an inky-black darkness that had all but suffocated him. So, sure. There were decisions. But the pearls had all been yanked well out of reach.

It was why getting used to anything...getting attached to *anyone*...always came with painful ramifications.

But this was Saoirse's story. He wanted to listen attentively and understand, for her. Everything about this moment seemed preserved in a special soundproof bubble wrapped around the

garden table they'd chosen in a quiet corner—
a bit of added protection against the hurt she'd
endured at another's selfish decision.

"So, anyway," Saoirse continued, after another
fortifying swig of margarita, "Tom—that's his
name. Feel free to hate it if you like, I do. Anyway, he had been my boyfriend since school
days. Off and on, like. You know how relationships are when you're young."

Santi nodded affirmatively but again found
he couldn't really say. His teenaged years had
been far from footloose and fancy-free. He forced
himself to tune back in.

"...and then when everyone coupled up or left
for the bright lights of Dublin, we started seeing
each other again. He became a policeman and
I became a nurse in the hospital up in the next
town along because our village was only tiny.
All our friends were getting married and so we
decided to get married."

"A mutual decision?"

"Sort of, I guess. I mean, he got down on one
knee and everything, but it all felt as if he was
going through some sort of pantomime version
of what a man who was in a relationship at a
certain age was meant to do when he proposed
to his girl."

"Weren't you in love with him?" Santi felt his
brows crowd together. This was hardly the portrait of a bewitched bride.

"Of course I was! At least, I thought I was." She twisted her lips as she considered the question. "I was as in love with him as much as a girl who's only known one boy her entire life could be. We met when I pushed him off the swings at school." Her eyes took on a faraway look as she gave a mirthless laugh. "He was the same boy I had my first kiss with and saw my first film alongside and just about everything else in the first department."

She waved off Santi's sympathetic murmurs. The proverbial floodgates were open now and there was no stopping this story. Not that he wanted her to stop. They'd spent over eighty working hours together over the past week and he hadn't even perfected saying her first name, let alone learned much about her other than that she had an unquenchable passion for race car driving.

"So, to turn a long story into a short one—because I'm guessing you don't want to hear every revolting detail of my childhood romance…"

He nodded. The more she told him, the more protective he was feeling about her. And not in a big-brother way.

"Our big plan was always to come over to America. Maybe that's the only thing we had in common. A desire to flatten our vowels and strive for more in the land of opportunity!"

"I thought you said this was the short version." Santi grinned, grabbing a handful of chips.

"Right you are." She nodded. "Instead of getting married straight away, we lived together and all, but our lives were dedicated to scrimping and saving and preparing for the Great American Adventure." She held her hands up and made a little ta-da trumpet sound.

This had been a long-term relationship. Would the recovery take as long as the relationship itself? Santi filed the information away.

"When exactly did you come over?"

"Tom came over first. About a year ago."

Ah! A chink. He stopped the swarm of judgments forming. This wasn't a moment to rub your hands together in glee because all had not been as it seemed.

"He got his green card through a relative already living in Boston. I suggested we get the fiancée visa thing right away, but practical Tom said no—we wouldn't have enough money while he was in the academy and I couldn't work straight away, so we should wait until we were married properly. I came out and visited him, but he was super busy all the time and nurse's wages don't go far, so I spent a lot of time in the library where I discovered I could come over on a student visa and not bother about the whole fiancée thing. I was tired of my life being in a holding pattern, you know?"

Santi didn't think he was meant to answer, but gave her a decisive nod. He *did* know. Caring for Alejandro after his lifesaving transplant surgery hadn't been a hardship, but to teenaged Santiago? It had felt like being chained to a life he'd never signed up for. Joining the Marines had seemed the only way to loosen the noose of hard-core responsibility he and his brothers had been forced to accept.

"So to make this really long story even pithier, I started raking around and eventually found a specialist NICU training course that would sponsor me. Taking it would put me well above the other NICU nurses if we ever decided to go back home to Ireland."

Santi tried not to wince each time she said "we" or "home." As she continued, the basket of tortillas became more and more interesting to him. If she were to see the look in his eyes, she would see glimpses of the green-eyed monster.

"This was all before Tom flew back for his summer holidays and our wedding. Then, as part of the health check for the visas, I found out I couldn't have children." Her voice went flat as she continued, as if giving the words their intended punch would make them impossible to say. "A month later I was standing in a stupid white dress all by my lonesome with a huge fruitcake no one wanted to eat." She plastered on a bright smile. "So I switched courses, joined the paramedic training course, chopped off my hair and moved to Miami because it's about as different from Boston as you can get. I wasn't going to give up all my dreams just because I'd chosen badly in the fiancé department. Now my visa's set to run out when my training ends and the only way I can stay without leaving is to get married. Happy?"

The look she gave him—one mixed with innocence, hope, confusion and sadness—all but yanked Santi's heart straight out of his chest. He could translate the depth of feeling to what he felt for his brothers, but the difference in their situations was vital. He'd been the one to leave them in the lurch. He'd been the Tom in the situation. Santi made a quick search for the invisible waitress, suddenly wishing he'd ordered a drink, as well. Water and iced tea weren't cutting it anymore.

He scrubbed a hand through his hair, firmly reminding himself this was Saoirse's time. He was doing this for her.

One selfless act.

It was all he wanted to see himself do before he reentered his brothers' lives.

If a priest walked through the door right now? He was in. If she wanted him to marry her, he would. But she would have to be sure she could accept what he had to offer: absolutely nothing.

"Do you mind if I ask about your fertility issues?"

"What, nurse-to-doctor-style?" She drew away from him as she spoke.

"Friend to friend," he replied.

Her shoulders softened. It wasn't an inquisition.

"In for a penny…" she halfheartedly quipped, swiping at some tears. "The doctors weren't entirely sure. I'd always had an irregular cycle so I mentioned it to the doctor who was doing the physical. It was more precautionary than exploratory, you know? And then the tests came back." She gave the picnic table an unhappy rap with her knuckles. "The details are a bit blurry now, partly because I burned the papers after my ex left. But apart from having an abnormally shaped uterus… Yeah, I know," she said when he widened his eyes, "there was more. Something about not ovulating regularly and not having a massive store of eggs. I wasn't really taking it all in with the wedding plans and sorting out my course and packing up the flat… It just——" Her voice broke ever so slightly. "The gist of it was that I'd be better off looking into adoption or having a surrogate or donor eggs—all things I knew Tom would never agree to."

"Sounds to me like he found someone else

when he was in the US and chose the coward's way out."

Saoirse's eyes went wide, the clear blue clouding with a fresh film of emotion.

"What did you say?"

"Sorry—it's not my place, I know. But from where I'm sitting, it just sounds to me like he'd found someone else, or chickened out, or—"

"Are you saying he would've left me, no matter what?"

Santi shredded three paper napkins in quick succession in an effort to stop himself from reaching out to Saoirse, providing the comfort he'd longed for when his mother had died in front of him. A near primal need overtook him to wipe away the tears spilling onto her cheeks, cup her soft cheek in his hand and tell her everything would be all right, but he knew it would be a lie. Most things that hurt you that badly were never all right again. He was living, breathing proof.

"Forget I said anything. If he told you it was for the infertility—" He could've punched himself in the head. Why did he have to open his big fat stupid mouth?

"He never said anything. I just…" Her voice faltered. "I just assumed that's what it was."

"It sounds like you're better off without him either way," Santi said, hearing the defensiveness in his own voice. Since when had he become Chief Saoirse Protector?

"Yeah." She nodded limply. "Sounds like it."

His heart went out to her. To find out she couldn't have children when she'd so clearly seen being a mother in her future and then to be publicly humiliated for her body's betrayal... No wonder she'd been devastated.

Particularly when the woman all but oozed life. She would have made an incredible mother. Vibrant, full of life, passionate. Just like his. He closed his eyes for a moment, an image of his own mother coming in and out of focus as well as memory would allow.

She'd been so brave. Picking up and leaving her homeland with her young husband after losing two babies in pregnancy owing to poor medical facilities. Wanting more for the children they hoped to have one day than their country could offer. Giving up their professional dreams for the steady income from the bodega when getting other jobs proved next to impossible. The sacrifice of it all. The *selflessness*.

Marrying Saoirse might be helping her, but from where he was sitting it served him every bit as much as it served her. So if they were going to do this he needed to know she was solid that this was exactly what she wanted. He wasn't in it for love or the twentieth-anniversary parties or long-lasting honeymoon periods. He was in it to pin himself to Miami, where he had some debts to pay.

"*Dulzera.* Sweetheart." Santi edged away the bowl of salsa resting between them and took her hands in his. "Does being here in Miami make you happy?"

"Very." She answered without a moment's hesitation.

"Why?"

"I feel…" She pulled her hands out of his, tucking them under her chin as her eyes flicked up to the fairy lights and palms and evening sky above them as if waiting for the answer to float down. She sucked in a huge breath and solidly met his gaze, "Believe it or not, I finally feel like *myself* here."

"You didn't like yourself in Ireland?" He carefully dodged the use of the word "home."

"Not particularly." She shook her head as if she were letting all the facts fall into place. "I used to have long hair, because that's what most of the girls I went to school with had. I used to wear ridiculous shoes out to even sillier nightclubs in the next town along because that's what everyone else did. Here? Here it takes me three seconds or less to fix my hair. I don't even bother with makeup," she added, as if it were the most liberating thing in the world. "And pony car racing. I did it at first to become better at driving the ambulance, what with the switch to the right side of the road and all, but… I *love* it." Her eyes took on a starry quality that immediately brought a smile to his lips. "I've got a race tomorrow. Do you want to come?"

"Absolutely." He nodded. "On one condition."

"What's that?" Saoirse asked, her entire demeanor suddenly lighter.

"You let me marry you and help you stay."

"Seriously?" There was more hope than wariness in her question this time.

"Seriously." If this wouldn't prove he was trying to turn over a new leaf, he didn't know what would. "It would be my pleasure."

"And the whole dead parents thing doesn't have anything to do with this?"

Her hands clapped over her mouth the second she said the words and he had to admit he had to catch his breath, too.

It was all well and good when he was the one "joking" about his issues, but coming from someone else? It hurt.

He slapped on a smile. This was all part of it. The good, the bad and the taking it on the chin.

"Nope!"

So it was a lie. But it was pretty clear she could see right through it and she was still holding on so…

"But…uh…" A flush crept onto her cheeks. "Just to be clear, there would be no nooky or making out in the back of cars at the drive-in or whatever it is you Americans get up to. Separate bedrooms, for sure. And no smelly socks!"

Back on the familiar turf of wisecracks and locker-room gibes, he regrouped. He nodded emphatically. "I can handle that."

Tempting as she was, Saoirse was laying down the guidelines. Keeping her heart safe from any more hurt. He would have to do the same. It was the only way this harebrained thing would work.

"Got it."

"And it only has to be two years, give or take an immigration inspection, and then you're free to run off and fall in love with whoever takes your fancy. Or I suppose if you do fall in love with someone in the meantime, then I could divorce you for being a lying cheat!" she concluded with a bit too much glee.

"What if I don't want to be a lying cheat?" he countered, contrarian that he was, before chomping down on a tortilla chip with a self-congratulatory smirk even he knew didn't make it all the way to his eyes. "What if I want to be as true as the blue on the American flag or the glorious Floridian skies above us?"

"That blue?" Her eyes widened.

"That blue." He nodded. He hadn't meant the sky or the flag this time around.

"Huh." She pursed her lips at him, adding in a dubious twist.

Thanks for the vote of confidence, sweetheart!

Her obvious lack of belief in his ability to commit stuck, thorn sharp, and almost instantly began to fester. He grabbed his shot glass, gave it a wiggle, disappointed he'd drained it the first time around.

"Santi, this is a big ask. I'm not going to hold you to it if you wake up in the morning and want to run for the hills."

All I want is a chance. A chance to do right by someone.

"Like I said, it's not a problem. I'm happy to do it."

She sat back, arms crossed, and huffed out a sigh. "Okay, fine. There's only one way I can be sure you really mean it."

"What's that, then?"

"Pinky promise."

He threw back his head and laughed. "That's the arbiter of whether or not you can take me at my word?"

"Yes. I need to be absolutely sure this wouldn't be cramping your style, or ruining your life, or making your world miserable, or that I'm putting one tortilla too many in your basket. Like Amanda said, this has to be a business deal."

Santi guffawed and put on a hokey cowboy accent. "Only if you don't go changin'."

"So you'll really do it?" Her shoulders relaxed a tiny bit and that hint of hope he liked to see returned to her eyes. "Even though I'm all hyper and overexcited and ready to tattoo *Miami Forever* on my backside if that's what it'll take?"

"No, you're good." He took a gentle swat at her chin with a paper napkin. "Especially with salsa hanging on your face in case we need some for later."

She nodded gravely. "I can do that for you, Santiago Valentino. Salsa on tap. Not a problem."

They both dissolved into another round of gut-clutching laughter, only just managing to calm themselves when the waitress reappeared, arms laden with plates holding *carnitas* and all the essential accoutrements. Hot-sauce heaven.

Santi dug in, suddenly ravenous. Hungry not only for the food but for the next day and the next, when his life would no longer be a solo voyage. Sure, a huge part of it was make-believe, but for all the pretense, what was growing between them felt *real*. Two lost souls trying to find their place in the world. Maybe this time it really would be here…home.

"Right, then," he said, after enjoying a savory mouthful of *carnitas*. "Guess we'd better start talking practicalities. Your place or mine?"

CHAPTER SIX

"So," AMANDA STARTED, all casual like, as if the tension in the air wasn't already almost palpable, "have you cleared out a couple of drawers?"

"Sort of."

"What do you mean, *sort of*?" She jumped up from the sofa. "Santiago's moving in. Today."

"It's all a bit fast, don't you think?" Turned out having a few nights on her own to think about things had been long enough to reopen the worrywart drawer Saoirse had thought she'd nailed shut. Tense didn't even begin to cover how she was feeling.

"Cutting things to the wire is more like it." Amanda pressed her lips together as if it would help make her point. Saoirse was between a rock and a hard place and needed to quit trying to find an escape route.

"I know but don't you think...?" *It's a bit too real.* "Do you think he'll have his own furniture?"

"Oh, come on! The guy's a nomad. It'll be the

contents of his motorcycle panniers and nothing else." Amanda held up her hand as a visual tick list. "He lives in a serviced apartment. He's been overseas for, like, a decade or something with the Marines. He probably didn't even have a tent he's so hard-core. I bet he wove himself a fresh duvet out of swamp reeds every night, taking shelter in the crook of a solitary oak tree." Her eyes took on a faraway look that didn't look altogether faithful to her own husband.

"I hope you're not daydreaming about my future husband," Saoirse half joked. "And I don't think there's an abundance of oak trees in Afghanistan." Amanda's eyes widened with amusement.

"I'm just messing with you, Saoirse. No need to get testy."

"I'm *not* getting testy," Saoirse replied...testily. "It's just—it's going to be a busy day."

"Yes, honey. You keep on telling yourself that, but I think someone's got a crush on her arranged-marriage husband!" Amanda's grin was so self-satisfied there'd be no wiping that thing off her face. Saoirse glared. It was all she had left in her armory of rebuttals.

"Point being, Murph, he doesn't have squat. He needs you as much as you need him."

"I think I'm going to have to disagree with you there, Amanda." Saoirse tried to put on her own comedy voice, but felt the truth of her statement weight her feet to the floor. Santi didn't need to marry her. At all. She was the only beggar in this scenario.

"Oh, come on! Look at all of the pluses. You two meet on the job, then at Mad Ron's where I bet you any amount of money he was hoping to find you. The two of you hit it off right away and now—ta-da! We've got a groom! We've got a plan! I just need to book a date down at the courthouse as soon as you fill out the paperwork, which…" she pushed a piece of paper across the coffee table "…I have generously printed out for you here. And I think I'll put in an order for those coconut cupcakes you like so much. Want to have a bridal shower?"

Saoirse scowled.

"Okay—maybe not. But c'mon, Murph," her friend lovingly wheedled. "Planning your Big Fat Fake Wedding is going to be wicked awesome!" Amanda could barely contain her excitement.

"Who says that sort of thing? 'Wicked awesome'?" Saoirse grinned, despite herself. The antiwedding wedding. It could work.

She put the paper on the breakfast bar and started hacking at some avocados to make her version of guacamole. Even though the situation was all a bit mad, Santi's rescue mission had relieved a massive load of tension.

"People from Boston," Amanda riposted, then immediately tried to stuff the words back into her mouth. "Sorry, sorry. I know I shouldn't mention Boston." She handed Saoirse a lime. "Here, squeeze some of that in. Keeps it from going brown."

"Thanks. And don't worry about the Boston thing. You can't help where you're from." Saoirse mashed the avocados a bit more aggressively than was strictly necessary. "I probably shouldn't hate a city forever just because it has one devious ex lurking around its thoroughfares."

"And you know for sure he's there?" Amanda started fastidiously folding paper napkins as if they were preparing to host the First Lady and not just four people for an alfresco lunch.

"I know he finished at the academy so I guess he's busy laying down the law in Boston by now."

Amanda arced a curious eyebrow.

"My parents. They keep me up to date with the news in jolly little emails designed, I am quite sure, to have life go back to normal, i.e., the good ol' days of Saoirse and Tom."

"They're still rooting for him after what he did?"

"They…" Saoirse pushed the bowl of smashed avocado away and began chopping tomatoes into itsy-bitsy cubes. "They want their little girl back."

"But I thought you and Tom were going to live in America."

"Yeah, sure, but—I don't know. I suppose they

played along but were convinced once we had children we'd come back. And now they're not so sure anymore." She gave Amanda a quick glance before returning to work. "I'm not the Saoirse I was nine months ago, am I? I mean, if you'd told me then I was going to have short, sun-bleached hair, would be driving an ambulance *and* going to racing school, not to mention marrying a superhot doctor I'll have to pretend I haven't pictured naked just to stay in Miami, I would have told you that you were stark raving—"

"You've pictured me naked?"

Santi appeared in the open French doors that led to her tiny backyard, holding a barbecue in his hands. It made his biceps stand out that perfect amount of sexy.

It was far too easy to picture Santi naked. Or wrapped only in a towel, little droplets of shower water still clinging to his—

She clenched the edge of the counter to disguise her knee-wobble.

"Yeah, right, hombre! In your dreams."

Even blind people would have the hots for Santi. His scent was every bit as scrumptious as his aesthetics.

"Where do you want this thing?" Santi's satisfied grin proved he knew she was telling porky-pies.

"Wherever there's space. It's not as if I've got acres of land to choose from."

"Better than the two-by-four balcony off my sad excuse of an apartment."

"The place you're giving up, right?" Amanda chimed in, reminding them both they had agreed to live in Saoirse's not-very-large bungalow by the sea.

"Yes, ma'am." Santi returned to the French doors, gave Amanda a salute then leaned against the door frame, the sun outlining him as if he was heaven sent. His eyes scanned Saoirse's sparsely decorated bungalow. She hadn't really bothered nesting in the few months she'd lived here. Too much of a risk given the circumstances. She chose to call the minimalist look beach chic.

"Nice zebra rug." The look he threw her was a bit more Tarzan than she could bear. It was far too easy to imagine whipping up a dress out of the faux hide and swinging through the jungle to some treetop love nest.

"It's fake." Saoirse looked away. Just like their marriage would be.

"As discussed," Santi continued, oblivious to her all-too-real ogling, "I'm happy to move in tonight if you like."

"Sounds good." Amanda answered for her, then noticed her friend's fastidious muteness. "Right, Murph?"

"Yes, fine. Sure. Whatever's convenient." *Chop, chop, chop.*

"Wow!" Santi said drily, slipping one of her

breakfast bar stools between his legs without so much as a toe-rise. "Don't get excited or anything, *mi amor.*"

Saoirse tore her eyes away from him and reduced the tomato pieces to pulp.

Tall, sexy, straddled motorcycles and bar stools like a seasoned cowboy... The man was ticking so many boxes it was unreal! Not for the first time she wished she could meet his parents. See who had crafted this living statue of perfection. But, she reminded herself as she accidentally sliced into her finger with a yelp, if she could meet his parents Santi most likely wouldn't be all messed up and willing to marry her. Only a man with issues up the wazoo would be playing along with this nutty plan.

"Hey." Santi reached across and pulled her finger out of her mouth. "Let me have a look at that."

"Aw..." Amanda sighed. "Look at the two of you, all lovey-dovey."

"Hardly." Saoirse tugged her hand out of Santi's. "It's a microscopic cut. I think I'll survive."

"You tink so, do ya?"

"Don't mock my accent, I won't mock yours."

"I am not the one with the accent, missy. Just remember who's got the US passport in this scenario."

Santi received a glowering look in return.

"Thanks for the reminder."

"Make sure you wash that finger thoroughly," Santi cautioned, completely unrepentant. "And put a bandage on it. Plaster. Whatever you call them."

"For heaven's sake, you'd think I was lyin' on the floor, bleedin' to death, the way you're carrying on."

"What? I'm not allowed to care if my beloved fiancée has been injured?"

"Not with a Cheshire-cat grin the size of the Atlantic Ocean on your face, no!"

"I think I'll just run out to the store and grab some more lemonade before James arrives," Amanda said none too subtly, not that Saoirse or Santi showed any signs of breaking away from their standoff to bid her a fond farewell.

When the door clicked shut, Santi relaxed his pose, patting the stool beside him. "C'mere. I want to talk to you."

"Can't. I'm busy." Saoirse made a quick show of chopping things.

"Murph!" Santi growled. "Take a pew! Now."

Saoirse let the knife clatter to the counter, grabbed a paper towel to wrap around her bleeding finger and stomped over to the breakfast bar stool. It was suddenly annoying that she had to clamber onto the thing, unlike Santi's smooth move. Her height was not to her advantage.

"Right, then. What's got the hornets' nest all

stirred up today? I thought we'd agreed to do this thing."

Saoirse bridled. Was the man bereft of human emotions? Who just agreed willy-nilly to marry a virtual stranger? No strings. No nooky. No running a finger along the outline of the mouth she could hardly stop staring at.

"We did agree," she finally conceded. "And I'm grateful to you and everything, but..." *What if I fall in love with you? I can't do unrequited love. I can't do love.*

"Are you worried about me staying here with you? Cramping your style?"

"No," she answered, too quickly.

"From what I understand, it's important we make a show of having built a life together before we tie the knot, and what did you say we have—about two or three months?"

She nodded, her insides all but shriveling up with mortification.

"So...couples fall in love at first sight all the time. Right?"

Saoirse squirmed. She wasn't in love with Santi—she hardly knew the guy—but there was a connection. A chemistry that was getting harder to squelch. And chasing up a disaster of a nonwedding with an unrequited marriage of con-*visa*-enience? No, thank you! She'd rather get deported.

Santi took her hand in his and gave it a little

rub with his thumb before inspecting her finger as he spoke. It felt nice. Too nice. She feigned indifference as she listened.

"It's a question of practicalities, right?"

"Of course," she agreed in her fake happy voice.

Indifference wasn't working.

She pulled her finger out of his hand and wrapped it in a fresh paper towel. Whenever he touched her she felt all zingy, and *zingy* was not practical.

"Point A—" Santi tried a new tack, his voice the height of military efficiency. "I live in a place that's easy enough to give up. You have a lease for the next three months, if I'm not mistaken. It makes sense for me to come here and I promise I won't take up much shelf space in the bathroom, all right?"

Saoirse nodded, rather unsuccessfully fighting the arrival of a sting of tears. She closed her eyes and tipped her chin up. *Why was this so hard?*

She felt Santi's crooked index finger swipe at another tear, hardly a challenge now that they were freely tumbling down her cheeks.

"*Amor*, don't." He gently pulled her off her stool and tugged her into his arms. "Don't cry."

In his arms, she felt safer than she could have imagined. Free to cry, free to feel the push and shove of conflicting emotions. If this—this connection she felt—was real, she could imagine wanting to marry him in a heartbeat. And that was a problem.

Saoirse trembled when she felt his hands cup her face. *Don't mess this up now... This is your chance to make at least one of your dreams come true.*

She forced herself to open her eyes to meet his. The gold flecks amid the chicory darkness of his irises made him appear more leonine than ever before. A proud Latino man, earthily aware of his physical prowess. There was heat in his gaze. A muscle twitched in his jaw. The cut of his cheekbones all but drew pointy arrows to his full, sensual mouth. She flushed when she realized she'd been licking her lips.

She searched for answers to the parade of questions goose-stepping through her mind. Nothing useful presented itself. Just a single sentence repeating itself over and over... *I want to kiss you.*

"Is it your ex?" Santi asked. Her eyes were still firmly planted on his lips. "Do you want to patch things up with him? Is that it?"

She squinted up at him as if it would change the words that had just come out of his mouth. Talk about a mood killer! Or maybe there had been no mood at all. Just a Saoirse-Santi romance mirage.

Then again...she chanced a glance at his eyes. No. It wasn't his eyes. The man was a trained

Marine. It was his tone that had caught her attention. It sounded almost… Wait a minute. Was he *jealous* that she might want the lying, faithless no-goodnik back in her life? Or *relieved*? Either way she knew the answer.

"No," she answered solidly, not quite ready to step away from the warmth of Santi's embrace. One of his hands was resting loosely on her waist, the other on her shoulder, occasionally moving up to her cheek to wipe away some tears. Just the size of his hands, the softness of his touch made her feel so *feminine*. She'd never admit it, but it felt good. Powerful, almost. The closest she'd ever get to feeling like an Amazon queen.

Leaning in to kiss him would be so easy.

Pressing her cheek into his hand to absorb some of the comfort it gave, she became aware her eyes were still unable to resist the magnetic lure of his lips. She bit down on her own lower lip, fighting the desire to go up on tippy-toe, just a little bit, and taste…

"Don't do that," Santi said, abruptly pulling back.

"What?"

"That…lip thing you do."

"What lip thing?"

"There." He pointed at her mouth. "You're doing it right now."

"No, I'm not!" She did a few moves to try and

figure out what she'd been doing, highly aware that Santi's hands were still touching her, almost territorially. Nerves won out over a limitless supply of sultry choices she could have made. "You mean my buck teeth overbite thing?"

"*Mija.* You do not have buck teeth or an overbite." Santi's voice was gravelly, intense. Which made her stare at his lips even more. Sensual, full lips he was dragging a tooth along.

"Well," she huffed. "You do a lip thing, too!"

"No, I don't!" Santi looked at her as if she had just gone directly around the bend.

"Yes." She nodded soberly. "You do. It's all slow-motion and sexy and, for the record, extremely distracting."

"Oh, yeah?" Santi's mood and voice shifted again, slamming straight out of neutral into for-bedroom-only gear. Her tummy went all swoopy, melty, lava lamp on her. Oh, no, no, no… This was the so-bad-it-was-good sort of thing she'd heard about from friends of hers who'd settled down—or just plain old settled in her case.

Her eyes were magnetically drawn to his lips.

Beware! Beware the most perfect lips in the whole of Miami.

Her breath became jagged and uncontrollable. *He did the lip thing.* Saoirse had no choice.

She went up on tiptoe and kissed him.

From the moment her lips touched his she

didn't have a single lucid thought. Her brain all but exploded in a vain attempt to unravel the quick-fire sensations. Heat, passion, need, longing, sweet and tangy all jumbled together in one beautiful confirmation that his lips were every bit as kissable as she'd thought they might be.

Snippets of what was actually happening were hitting her in blips of delayed replay.

Her fingers tangled in his silky, soft hair. Santi's wide hands tugged her in tight, right at the small of her back. There was no doubting his body's response to her now. The heated pleasure she felt when one of his hands slipped under her T-shirt elicited an undiluted moan of pleasure. He matched her move for move as if they had been made for one another. Her body's reaction to his felt akin to hitting all hundred watts her body was capable of for the very first time.

She wanted more.

No.

She wanted it *all*. The whole package. The feelings. The pitter-patter of her heart. Knowing it was reciprocated. Being part of a shared love. Not some sham wedding so she wouldn't have to live in a country where her soul had all but shriveled up and died.

She felt Santi's kisses deepen and her willpower to shore up some sort of resistance to what was happening plummeted. This felt so *real*. And a little too close to everything she'd hoped for wrapped up in a too-good-to-be-true package. This sort of thing didn't happen to her. And it wasn't. She'd started it, Santi was just responding. She heard herself moan and with its escape her resolve to resist abandoned her completely.

She caved in to her body's desires. To caress and be caressed. Explore and discover new ways of giving pleasure. Time and space and heat and light all melded into one as she felt her body blossom with sensation after sensation. Each and every one of them pure pleasure.

The sharp jangle of her phone's text alert shot through her body just as she was weaving one bare leg around Santi's.

They both froze, eyes wide as if the neighborhood priest had just walked in on the pair of them, clothes asunder, tousled hair, hot, heated pants of desire slowing as they let reality settle around them.

Bzzt!

Saoirse batted her hand around the counter without changing her position and finally found purchase on the phone. She brought it up to her eyes, blocking out Santi's amused expression.

Lovers' quarrel over? Safe to come back now? We are ten minutes away, can delay if necessary. xx A

At least it was proof Amanda hadn't installed a secret camera anywhere.

"Amanda?" Santi asked, tipping his head out from behind the screen of her smartphone.

"Amanda." Saoirse's thumb tapped away at the phone, telling her to hurry up, suddenly aware how close she'd come to giving herself, body and soul, to Santi.

"Tell her the barbecue's off," Santi murmured, his hands slipping around her waist, trying to close the space that had opened up between them.

"No. Sorry." She pressed a hand against his chest, forcing herself to wriggle out of his embrace, swiping a hand over her kiss-bruised lips as she did. "I think that's probably enough of that. We made a rule. Remember?"

Rich, coming from the number one rule breaker.

She pulled her glass of iced tea along the countertop, leaving a watery pool in its wake, and took several long slurps through her pink flamingo straw. It was one of the first purchases she'd made when she'd moved here, kitting her house out with dollar-store specials, and it never failed to make her smile. She hardly noticed it now. She needed the icy tea to tamp down the flames of desire licking away at her nerve endings in wicked little flicks and quivers.

"Want some?" She held the glass out to Santi.

He shook his head, eyes clouded with something she couldn't quite read. Irritation? Or ardor?

"James and Amanda are going to be back in a few minutes, yeah?"

Saoirse nodded. Where was this going?

"And James is going to talk us through the whole process—the legal process—of putting in the forms for you to stay here and what we'll have to prove and show, et cetera, right?"

Gulp. He wasn't going to back out, was he? Or maybe he should. Friends only was one thing, but friends with benefits? That had red, hot and dangerous written all over it.

"Yeah." She nodded, fingers unable to resist touching her kiss-swollen lips again. *Could lips pine for someone else's?*

"Amanda and James thought this barbecue was a good way to introduce the formal factor into the proceedings. Make the whole thing a bit more relaxed."

"Are you relaxed?" Santi's body tensed as he spoke, evoking a jangle of nerves in her own.

"Not exactly."

It wasn't exactly a declaration of love but at the very least he knew he was now officially under her skin.

Santi gave his shoulders a sharp shake, eyes closed tight as he tried to clear his head of all the behind-closed-doors things he wished he was doing to Saoirse right now. She'd felt good in his arms, pressed against his body, wanting him as much as he now knew he wanted her. There was a pool of sunshine on the wide-planked wooden floor he wouldn't mind laying her out in. Slowly…luxuriously…stripping off her tomboy gear and making it incredibly clear just how desirable he thought she was.

Válgame Dios!

What was life throwing him now? A buoy or an anvil that would shunt him straight to the bottom of the sea?

He wasn't doing a very good job of proving he could be steady, reliable. The whole point of this exercise.

He opened his eyes, forcing his features and voice into a neutral zone the rest of him wasn't quite yet in.

"We should be. Relaxed *and* happy. This is a big decision. For both of us, eh, *dulzera*?" He ducked his head in a vain attempt to catch Saoirse's blue eyes with his. In his gut—hell, in his *heart*—he really wanted to do this for her, but only if they could both leave unscathed at the end. "I'm afraid the ball's in your court for this one, Murph. It's your call. If I'm not the guy for you, there's no point in me moving in here and going through this whole charade."

She shifted uncomfortably, eyes skidding everywhere around the room but on him.

"I guess it's the part about it being a charade that I'm not really comfortable with, you know? That it's fake."

"I don't know about you, but what just happened didn't feel so fake to me."

"I know! That's exactly my point!"

"I don't follow."

"It's just that…" Saoirse only just stopped herself from tracing a heart shape onto his chest.

It'd be too easy to fall in love.

"Maybe it's so close to the other wedding—you know, the Irish one—that I've got some guilt or…"

Saoirse trailed off, not sounding convinced by her own argument. Santi had little doubt she was over her ex and from the kisses she'd just been giving him? No, it wasn't guilt.

"I just feel a bit duplicitous. It's a shame it's not—you know…"

"The real thing?" He finished for her.

"Yes." She nodded glumly. "It would have been nice if our—*the* marriage was for real."

He nodded. He knew what she meant. But setting things right with his brothers was his priority. And so far coming back to Miami was the only step he'd taken in that direction. Getting married for real before he was square with his brothers simply wasn't going to happen.

"It would have been nice, but unless a messed-up ex-Marine is your thing…" He ignored the sharp glance she gave him. One filled with questions. Questions he wasn't ready to answer.

There was no point in going into details. The fact he couldn't, with any sort of clean conscience, give his heart to her was the main thing they had going for them. She'd see soon enough. Friends was great. More than that? Not worth the trouble. There'd be another guy, another day... He just needed to see that smile of hers again. It lit him up, more than he liked, but that would be his cross to bear, not hers.

"Murph, c'mere. Sit down." He patted her stool in a show of *It's-okay,-I won't-bite* and waited for her to climb back up, arms crossed, a leery expression playing across her features.

"We're friends, aren't we?"

She tilted her head to the side, pretending to size him up. "As much as a girl can be with a man who insists on scrunching saline bags between his shoulder and chin can be."

"It's how we always did it out in the field. And it's not like I have a hook on my head."

"We could install one," She hiccup-laughed, then smiled, visibly pleased he was playing along. As full of bravado as she was, he'd already learned Saoirse needed a bit of silly in her day to soften the edges of a life that hadn't been altogether kind to her, and he was more than happy to oblige.

"We could install a clip on your work cap. I'll call you Mr. Saline Head," she said, almost shyly.

"And you thought I was the mad one." Santi laughed, pleased to hear her giggling along with him. How quickly it had come to pass, he thought, that a smiling Saoirse was all the sunshine he needed.

"C'mon." He clapped his hands together and gave them a quick rub. "I meant what I said. I am completely happy to do this for you. The marriage thing. I know there'll be times where it will be tough. Days where we probably want to see the backside of each other—but that lends the whole thing a bit more authenticity, right?"

"I happen to have a very nice backside, thank you very much."

"I know."

Her cheeks colored as she realized just how recently his hands had been cupping said backside. Just as quickly she feigned a shocked gasp. "You won't be letting the cat out of the bag, will you? About the blubbing and the feelings and everything? I've got a tough-girl image to keep up at work."

"No, ma'am." He stood, clicked his heels together and gave a quick salute. "As long as you keep it close to your chest I've got a weak spot for…" *You.*

"*Carnitas* and zebra hides?" Saoirse suggested.

"Got it in one." He winked.

Emergency averted. Time to get back on course. Business only. Doing the right thing by someone. Soon. Soon, he'd do the same for his brothers. But that was going to take some staring-into-the-eyes-of-the-firing-squad courage. He didn't deserve their forgiveness. He didn't deserve their love. You had to earn that sort of thing and his bank balance in that department was more than likely running on empty.

"Right, Murph." He stood and gave her a brotherly shoulder hug with a play growl. "Let's see about getting this barbecue up and running before your pals come back, otherwise it's raw burgers and E. coli all around."

"On it." Saoirse hopped off her stool and headed toward the refrigerator, abruptly screeching to a halt. "Valentino?"

"Yes, Murphy?" he replied formally.

"You are a *good* friend."

Friend. He saw the invisible partition being placed between them and instantly wished it gone. *Friend.* Didn't seem to sit right somehow.

Well, too bad for him. He'd made his bed and now it was time to lie in it. In the spare room.

"Not everyone would make this big a commitment for nothing. Especially given…you know." She made a kissy face and a yucky face in quick succession, gave a little decisive nod and started humming as she yanked open the fridge door and started noodling around inside for the hamburger fixings.

He was glad she couldn't see the sad smile he knew was hitting his face about now. He wanted, more than anything, to be a good friend to Saoirse. He could just as easily see himself wanting a whole lot more. She was a singular woman who deserved to be loved. Love he couldn't give right now. Until he started tackling the promises he'd made to himself on the blood-soaked battlefields, he was no good to anyone. No one at all.

"Right." James eyed them as he would a jury. First Santi, from whom he received a curt nod. Then Saoirse, who had to stop herself from giggling.

"Are the waters muddy or clear on how this whole thing works?"

"Clear!" they said in unison, hands raising as if they had a body between them and were about to deliver an AED shock. Their eyes hooked at the "jinx" and they both dissolved into uncontrolled laughter.

"You're right, babe." James leaned over and gave his wife a kiss on the cheek. "They are a cute couple. You two won't have any problems. I see setups come through all the time and I can tell you're the genuine article."

Saoirse blinked a minute, trying to register his words. Santi seemed entirely unaffected by them and started peppering James with the best way to clean a barbecue grill.

The genuine article?

Saoirse looked across at Amanda, a veritable halo glowing around her she looked so happy. "You didn't tell him?" Saoirse mouthed.

Amanda shook her head, her grin widening as she did, then tipped her head in the direction of the kitchen.

"Why didn't you tell him this was fake?" Saoirse whispered when they reached the cool of the kitchen.

"No-brainer! I'm not getting my husband involved in something I think is shady." Amanda looked appalled. "Besides…" she smirked "…James sees exactly what I see."

"And what would that be? *Exactly?*" Saoirse's tone was filled with a bit more attitude than she'd intended.

"A spark. Lots of them," Amanda replied, giving the counter a swipe with a sponge as she did. "I've been watching you two ever since you met and, frankly, I'm surprised he hadn't already moved in."

"What? Are you crazy?"

"No," Amanda answered plainly. "There's a whole lotta me thinks the lady doth protest too much going on here. C'mon, Murph. You totally have the hots for that guy and, if I'm not mistaken, he wouldn't mind a little slice of Murphy pie either."

Saoirse glared at her friend. It was her only line of defense. Then blushed.

"*Sare*-shae! You naughty little so-and-so!"

"It's *Murphy*," Saoirse hiss-whispered, making a keep-your-voice-down hand gesture.

Amanda leaned against the kitchen counter and crossed her arms. "When are you going to stop this?"

"What?" She knew what Amanda was talking about, but decided rubbing at a nonexistent stain in the deep ceramic sink was more fruitful than playing along.

"Acting like you don't care. I've been trying to set you up for *months* and this is the first time you've bitten. Hook, line and sinker. And all of this pally-buddy stuff?"

"What pally-buddy stuff?" she snapped back defensively.

"Duh!" Amanda began raising a finger per point. "The spats. The arm punches. The high fives. The pretending you totally don't secretly love it every time he gives you knuckle-rubs because it gives you a chance to take a deep, lovely inhalation of his gorgeous cinnamon man scent. I could go on but I'm running out of fingers. Suffice it to say, Murph, you're fooling no one."

Saoirse opened her mouth to protest but nothing came out.

"Murph…the way you behave with Santi is the equivalent of shoving a boy in the playground because what you really want to do is kiss him. Admit it."

Saoirse squirmed under her friend's penetrating gaze.

"Okay, fine." She caved. "I kissed him."

"I knew I was right!" Amanda shouted, before remembering she was meant to be speaking under a cloak of secrecy, then stage-whispered, *"I'm always right,"* as if it erased the jubilant cry heard half the way to Brazil.

"What did you know, hon?" James called from the patio.

Saoirse pressed her hands together in prayer position and shook her head. *No-no-no.* Please don't tell.

"That Murph and Santi were hoping to get married on St. Patrick's Day." She hooked her arm through Saoirse's and steered her back out into the tiny garden, beaming as if she were announcing her own nuptials. "Isn't that cute? With Murphy being Irish and all?"

"Adorable," Santi replied, eyes more narrow than wide with Amanda's unexpected news flash.

There was a *date*?

If he'd thought moving into Saoirse's had been a reality check, a bona fide *wedding date* really punched it home.

He was going to have to make good with his brothers before then. Introducing them to his green-card bride without a bit of rift-fixing? Wasn't going to happen.

He did a mental scan through the year's calendar... St. Patrick's Day was about ten weeks away, by his calculations. Not a long engagement. Then again, his parents had met at a dance and had been engaged by the end of it, so by their terms?

Ten weeks had been a lifetime. A lifetime the two of them hadn't been able to share.

He cleared his throat. It was time to get the ball rolling.

Ten weeks was his new deadline to get things right with his brothers. He was sure they already thought he was nuts and adding this to his catalog of ill-advised life choices wasn't going to change the portrait.

"Well, then!" He watched as Saoirse put on her best hostess face. "Now that we're all caught up on each other's news, who's up for going along to the track with me for a bit of pony car racing?"

He, it appeared, wasn't the only one feeling the heat.

CHAPTER SEVEN

"HIGH FIVE!" SANTI held up his hand as she beamed at his obvious pride over his bride-to-be's panache at the wheel. She'd seriously messed it up today. The good-way kind of messing things up. Not her usual actual messing things up.

"C'mon!" He prodded when she didn't meet his hand. "High five!"

"Nah." She pulled off her helmet, shaking her pixie cut back into place. "We need a secret handshake. High fives are old-school."

"I like your style, Murph." He nodded appreciatively before raising a finger of objection. "I get to pick it, though. Seeing as you shanghaied our wedding date."

"That was a week ago. Aren't you over it yet?" Saoirse teased, then gave a resigned shrug. "Amanda's a force of nature. I was powerless to resist. And I'm afraid the date is within the time-line we need to follow if the goal is to keep me in the country." She tugged her fingers through her hair and tossed her helmet into the seat of her old beater. Signing up for race car driving was one of the best things she'd done since moving here. Amazing the amount of stress you could release by careening around a chicane without touching the brake pedal.

"Don't worry, *mija*. The timeline is fine. The goal is still the same." Santi came around to her side of the car and without so much as a how-do-you-do tugged down the zip on her race jumpsuit in one fluid move.

He may as well have slipped his hands inside the suit and caressed her bare skin for the impact it had. Her skin soared directly into hypersensitivity mode, little tingly shots of electricity bringing parts of her back to life she'd thought were long dormant. Her heart was skipping beats like it was going out of style. As she looked up into those gold-flecked eyes of his, she realized he was probably watching her pupils dilate, betraying her body's response to his proximity. From a distance he was difficult enough to block out. Here? Not more than a few inches apart? *Oh, for the love of a cashmere sweater...* His stubble looked...*soft*.

So much for all that hard-won concentration.

"You're not going to try to dye the champagne green or anything, are you?" Santi's eyes twinkled as he looked down at her.

"Obviously! It's an Irish tradition." She took a

couple of steps back from him, feeling a serious need to regain a semblance of control.

Champagne? How seriously was he taking this thing? "If you're planning on inviting family, we can always have it on Cinco de Mayo or something. It'd be pushing things a bit from the paperwork end of things for me, but if we applied for a fiancée visa or I got an extension on—"

"No, no. St. Patrick's Day is fine."

Today would be fine.

"And it'll be just you and me," he added. No family. Not yet anyway.

"Against the world?" she added, her brow crinkling in a mirror image of his own, he suspected.

Family.

How could such a small word be so...loaded?

Santi took a couple of steps back himself. He wasn't the only one feeling the perfection of proximity. Or the danger.

He'd realized it an hour ago, watching her driving around the track, face lit up like it was Christmas morning as she'd deftly swerved and veered her way around the course, him in the passenger seat wondering who had made this woman so courageous and *real.* He was not a passenger-seat kind of guy—and yet? Here he was, happy to go along for the ride.

They clicked. On so many levels they clicked and day by day it was growing harder to pretend he was just a nice guy doing a nice girl a favor. Never mind the fact that sleeping in the spare room was just an exercise in torture. Even more so now that he was finally accepting that everything he was feeling for Saoirse was adding up to one thing: love. And there was nothing brotherly about it.

Fast? Hell, yeah. But with a woman like this? Suffice it to say, if he'd been born in his father's day, he would've asked her to marry him by the end of the first dance.

Not that he had a clue what Saoirse was feeling. She didn't do anything slow and steady— or halfway, from what he could gather. Not after what she had been through. It was now-or-never time. For everything.

Was it the same for falling in love?

His initial offer might've been all nonchalant and devil-may-care but now? Now he'd marry her to keep her in the country *and* give himself a fighting chance to see if she felt the same way he did.

He looked away and up to the sky, where some cloud cover was threatening to mask the morning sun.

Who knew? Maybe this was what genuine arranged marriages were like. Someone saw they were a good potential match, made it, and then it was up to the couple to make good on the potential. Or maybe he was just thinking too damn much about everything because Saoirse made him horny and there wasn't a thing he could do about it. Love wasn't only patient and kind. Love was a pain in the butt.

"At the risk of doing the nagging-wife thing a bit early..." Saoirse went on tiptoe to catch his attention, then looked away when she knew she had it, "Are you actually ever going to call your brothers?"

He had a little set-to with his hackles before answering as neutrally as he could. Like he'd said...pain in the butt.

"Don't worry. I'll call." Or drop by. *And leg it off to the Keys for a long-overdue ride to try and get my head straight.*

"Because it's weird going into the ER and panicking I'm going to see them."

"Don't worry about it. They're not ER kind of guys and generally not Seaside guys. They're at Buena Vista more often than not." From what he'd heard, anyway. His brothers had cut some serious pathways into each of their surgical specialties. He felt proud. From-a-distance pride.

"That was a freakish one-off, but don't worry. I'll tell them about you. Us." Her eye roll was too big to miss.

All right! It was a fib. He meant to. And yet each day that passed made the next one harder. Especially when he knew all he needed to do was pick up the phone and get on with it. Make peace to find peace.

He turned to see Saoirse give a little wiggle as she shrugged her shoulders out of her race suit, revealing a skimpy tank top skidding along the sides of her breasts. No need for imagination.

"¡Caracoles!"

"What was that?" Saoirse threw him a wary look.

"Nada."

The opposite of nothing was more like it.

He stuffed his hands in his pockets as she continued peeling off the jumpsuit, revealing her petite body bit by bit, curve by swoop... *Por Dios!*

"Murph." He scanned the parking lot for a concession stand. "I'm going to get some water before we go to brunch. Want anything?"

"Hang on a minute, my beeper's going off." She threw him her backpack. "The work one. Can you check it?"

He tugged the pager off the black strap and looked.

He felt his own pager sending vibrations along the length of his belt. No guesses what the message was. He looked anyway and grimaced. Whatever it was, it wouldn't be pretty.

"Saddle up, Murph. There's been a big one."

"Are you sure we packed everything?" Saoirse threw Santi an anxious look.

"It's the Keys, Murph, not the moon."

He gave her leg a reassuring pat. From the

sounds of the traffic reports coming in like bullet fire on their radio, it wasn't going to be pretty.

Two dueling Jet-Skiers had been swerving in and out of coastal fog patches. One of the Jet Skis had exploded underneath the driver just as they'd approached a causeway. The blast had sent him flying onto the windshield of a car that had veered into oncoming weekend traffic. Thirty... maybe forty vehicles involved. Including an oil truck. Two fatalities had already been called in.

Saoirse had actually looked grateful when Santi had insisted on driving after her time out on the track. It took a lot of concentration to come out on top. Energy she hadn't banked on saving for what could easily be a twenty-four-hour shift.

"I threw in a few extra of everything. There's always a supplies truck to follow up, as well. They'll call in county, the fire departments, everyone." He tried to dismiss the grim expression taking hold of his features. No point in giving her the jitters before they even got there. "The triage areas might already be set up by the time we get out there." He flicked the sirens off and on again to give a particularly pointed signal to the oblivious car in front of them.

"I suppose this sort of thing is your area of expertise," Saoirse said after a few minutes of silent weaving in and out of traffic. Sirens were sounding from all sectors of the city and cars were pulling to the side of the road well in advance, as if a statewide alert had been sounded. Doubtless the news was all over the radio.

"Accidents are just that." He pressed his lips together, hands gripping the wheel so tightly the veins strained against his skin. He'd done several tours in the military and each one had chipped away at his ability to stay neutral.

War was ugly. Ugly because it was intentional. Accidents? No one meant for them to happen. Throwing a grenade or setting off a shoulder-launched missile? There was nothing mistaken about that. And the lives lost? Just as pointless as the teenaged boys proving themselves to get into a gang by killing his parents.

A cruel waste. It was the spur that had finally pushed him to come home. Not that he'd made any headway in extending an olive branch to his brothers. War, it seemed, came more easily to him than asking forgiveness.

"You all right?"

"Fine, *querida*." He shot her a quick glance and gave her leg a quick pat. She was unwittingly becoming better and better at noticing when his thoughts drifted in the direction of his brothers. "Just getting in the right mind-set. And remember, we're a team. I've got your back."

She nodded silently, eyes glued to the road ahead of them.

"You've not been involved in an MCI before?"

"A Mass Casualty Incident? No."

"There are a lot of acronyms on days like this. You remember the START model, right? Things are a bit different in the military—but there's a lot of overlap. Okay—START." Santi kept his voice steady. He was used to being cool in dangerous situations. The more intense the fighting, the calmer he'd become. Maybe that was why the happier he felt with Saoirse, the more agitated he was feeling.

"START," Saoirse repeated, as if reading from a textbook. "Simple Triage and Rapid Treatment." She held up four fingers, bending them down as she went through each group. "The expectant. In other words, those who are likely to die. The injured who can be helped by immediate transportation. The injured whose transport can wait and people with minor injuries."

"See! You've got it. Priorities for evacuation and transport?"

"Deceased remain where they fall. Black tags—those expected to die within ten minutes or less are given palliative care to reduce suffering, but are likely to die of their injuries." Her voice became more clinical as she continued. He understood. It was vital to separate emotions from actions at times like these. She sucked in a breath and continued. "Immediate evacuation for the red tags—medevac if possible. Do you think they'll come? The helicopters?" She turned in her seat to face him.

"Absolutely. They're probably en route already. Keep going," he said, encouraged to hear her voice becoming calmer the more she reminded herself how much she did know.

"Ah, delayed or yellow tags can have delayed evacuation—that is, they can't go until everyone who has critical injuries has been transported."

"And the green tags?"

"Last in line, but need constant checking in case their condition changes and they require re-triaging." She sat back with a triumphant smile, which immediately dropped from her face as the accident scene came into view.

Santi's low whistle reflected what she felt. Impressive was the wrong word to describe what they saw. Overwhelming was coming close.

The fog that had enshrouded the causeway was clearing to reveal something more akin to a horror scene. Passengers and drivers were staggering out of vehicles. A fuel truck was jackknifed across three lanes of traffic, flames reaching higher with each passing moment. A couple of fire trucks and a rescue team were already on-site, doing their best to clear people as far away from the fuel truck as possible, columns of black smoke scalding the sky above them. The scream and roar of their equipment releasing trapped passengers from their vehicles was all but drowning out the cries for help.

Santi pulled their ambulance onto the edge of the causeway at the direction of a stressed-looking sheriff.

"Where do you want us?"

"Check with the Fire Rescue Squad. They were here first and know their way around an MCI better than anyone."

Santi and Saoirse each shouldered medical run bags, putting as many supplies as they could on their wheeled gurney, and ran into the depths of the scene.

"Over here! We need someone on the red tags until the medevac arrives!" A paramedic from the fire crew directed them to a huge red sheet where four people were laid out and another was on approach. "Can you start here? Compound tib-fib, arterial bleed. I'm afraid you'll have to do the rest." And he ran off into the choking fug of smoke and flames.

Santi dropped to his knees next to the unconscious patient, signaling to Saoirse to do the same on the other side. She pulled out her flashlight and checked the man's pupils for dilation. Her wrist flicked first to one eye, then the next.

"Responsive."

"Good," Santi muttered, his gloved fingers seeking and immediately stemming the arterial bleed in the man's leg.

The compound fracture was so crudely exposed to the elements Saoirse nearly retched at the sight.

"Check airways, circulation." Santi's voice was steady. Reassuring. Exactly what she needed.

This was precisely what her paramedic training had prepared her for. The car racing. Moving to Miami in the first place without knowing a soul. A complete reinvention in order to handle every painful curveball life threw at her.

She looked into Santi's eyes and felt fortified by the understanding they held, as if his strength was flowing directly into her. They *would* get through this. Together.

"We can do this one of two ways." He reached across to his run bag and grabbed a clamp for the arterial bleed. "Can you get a drip going on this guy with some morphine in the bag?" Her hands flew into automatic pilot, working quickly, efficiently as she focused on what he was saying. "We can work through the patients together, like the A-team we are, or you can peel off on your own and call me if you need a hand."

Saoirse looked up for a millisecond to gather her thoughts. Her eyes didn't even have a chance to reach the heavens before the decision was made for her. "Sir! Stay where you are!" Seconds became nanoseconds as she swiftly checked she'd secured the saline drip for Santi's patient. "You good here?" She received a curt nod and was up and guiding a man with a massive head wound to the large tarp for severe traumas, all the while taking in just how bad the situation unfolding around them was.

Time took on an otherworldly quality.

Head wounds were downgraded; blood flow always made them look worse than they were. A perforated lung was stabilized as best she could before a helicopter crew whisked the teenaged girl away. On Santi's count, they stabilized then shifted a screaming middle-aged woman who'd seen her daughter being loaded onto the helicopter, the screams increasing as the extent of her pelvic injuries became clearer.

Saoirse saw herself as if from above, a whirling blur of activity matching medical supplies to patients. Neck braces. Splints. Sterile bandages. Change after change of gloves. Her stethoscope pressing to chest after chest. The sudden realization her own knees were bleeding after kneeling in glass while giving lifesaving compressions to a little boy. Heartbeat. None. Clear!

She watched as her fingers unwrapped hydrocolloidal dressing for a twenty-something woman who'd just been pulled out of a burning vehicle, inserting a saline drip, doing her best to stop the woman from going into shock as she cooled then dressed her burns, all the time murmuring soothing confirmations that she would get to a hospital. She would survive this.

A shift in the wind abruptly changed the tenor of the entire operation.

Flames, licking at the sky above them, abruptly veered toward the triage section, bringing the thick black smoke along with it and all but threatening to devour everything in its path. Sight, sound and especially smell were overwhelmed with the terrifying change of events.

She froze completely—the heat of the fire seemed to be sucking the very oxygen out of the air around her. Out of her peripheral vision Saoirse saw firefighters unleash streams of foam into the inferno, to little effect. Instinct took over. The need to survive and to help her patient took precedence.

She threw herself over her patient in an arc, only just managing to slip a space blanket between them, ironically staving off the hypothermia the burned woman might be prone to.

As she heard and felt the elements around them being fought with the incredible bravery of the fire crews, Saoirse was rocked by a revelation, then another and another. Each hit of understanding striking her in all-encompassing body blows.

With the kind of clarity one has after a weather front thunders down abruptly then shifts and clears, she saw her life for what it was. A massive move forward.

Her need to change her life had come not from

heart*break*, as she'd thought, but from a deeper place. Something that had craved change. Her very *essence* had fought to become the woman she was now. And for the first time in her life she liked what she thought she had come to embody.

A brave, slightly lippy, kind soul. She dared to open her eyes, urgently needing to see Santi. He had helped her reach this place, to gain the new-found confidence she couldn't have ever imagined having just nine short months ago.

Still hunched over her patient, she squinted against the soot and smoke of the accident scene. The winds had shifted again and the firefighters were mastering the blaze now. But her eyes still sought and at long last gained purchase on the only visual salve she needed... Santiago Valentino.

Santi's eyes met Saoirse's and the interchange of relief and untethered emotion was all but palpable. He ached to pull her into his arms, wipe the soot from her face, take her away from all of this and assure her she would always be safe as long as he lived. But there was more work to do.

He'd just begun securing a patient to a backboard when the flames threatened and he needed to act as swiftly as possible. This was one of those moments when he was grateful for his time in the military. Of course, external factors mattered, but it was amazing what a man could block out when someone's survival was utterly dependent on you. Warfare, at its worst, made this mass casualty pale in comparison. But each life was every bit as precious.

He jacked up his treatment on the man lying in front of him. He'd seen this type of injury too many times. Traumatic brain injury. Pupils— nonresponsive. He did as quick a gauge on the Glasgow Coma Scale as he could but there were too many factors yet to be explored to be precise.

"What do you need?" Saoirse appeared by his side.

"The whole nine yards," Santi replied grimly. "Looks like this poor guy was ejected through his windshield. Significant brain trauma. Pupils are nonresponsive." He held his fingers in front of the man's mouth. "Breathing is compromised."

"Shall I intubate?"

"Sooner rather than later. We don't want him having to fight hypoxia as well."

Saoirse deftly inserted the intubation kit and together they got a flow of oxygen running. Recovery would be long and hard for this man, if not impossible. But Santi was going to give him every shot he could to fight the odds.

Together they scored the man's physiological parameters and gauged his systolic blood pressure.

"He's going to need a good neurosurgeon," Saoirse said.

Santi nodded. He hoped, for this man's sake, he could afford the elite clinic where his brother Dante worked as a neurosurgeon. This guy would need the best and Dante did nothing by halves. "Go on." He pointed Saoirse in the direction of another patient being transferred to the critical section. There weren't enough hands on deck for buddying up.

"I need a helicopter now!"

It was impossible to know if his words had reached the right ears. So he repeated it, again and again, until he was hoarse and a flying doctor's flight suit appeared in his eye line.

Time to move to the next patient.

More paramedics arrived. Doctors stuck in the traffic jam raced to offer assistance, tugging on neoprene gloves as they ran. Injury after injury presented itself. Each time Santiago began to wonder if his body could handle lifting another backboarded patient onto a gurney, a chopper basket, or just lending an arm of support as he steered a patient through the crowd to a loved one…his eyes sought Saoirse's. The clear blue of her gaze was exactly the life-affirming medicine he needed. Her energy never seemed to abate. Her focus was intense, her manner calm, exacting. Precisely the type of woman anyone would want to have come to their rescue if they were lucky enough to be visited by an angel.

He shook his head and gave it a rough scrub

with the tips of his fingers. His feelings for Saoirse were launching out of his heart at rocket speed. He'd never understood the lure of settling down until now. Not that he imagined a life with her would be akin to hanging up his hat in the adventure department. Far from it. Life with Saoirse would be—

"Santiago?"

He saw the man approach, knew he'd said his name, but couldn't make the connection. Not at first.

And then it hit him. Harder than he could have imagined.

Detective Guillermo Alvarez. The first person on the scene after his parents had been shot and ultimately killed. The one man who had promised to find the *pendejos* who'd turned a robbery into a double homicide, nearly taking his kid brother in the process.

This man's appearance was just about the one thing that could shake his focus.

Well…his brothers could've walked out of the crowd. That would've done the trick, too, but…

"Santiago. I thought that was you. Long time no see. *Acere, que bola?*"

"Estoy pinchando." He stuck out his hand, which was met for a sound shake, all the time refusing to concede that seeing the fifty-something detective was rattling him to his very core.

"You signed up, didn't you?" The detective

looked up to the sky as if a plane were going to fly by with the answer.

"Marines." Santi saved him the time.

"Sí, correcto." The detective nodded along. "Your brother—I think it was Alejandro who told me."

Santi kept his gaze level. How could he tell this man he hadn't seen his own brother since he'd been back, weighed down by over a decade of guilt and unfulfilled responsibility?

"Man, is he ever doing well. A pediatric transplant surgeon! Who would've thought it, eh? After all he'd been through? Working in a hospital would've been the last thing I would've wanted after going through what he had..." The detective's voice petered out, but Santi could have easily filled in the rest. The chain of events following the shootings were as alive in his mind as if they'd happened yesterday.

Santi scrubbed a hand over his face, hoping it came across as a gesture of pride rather than regret. What had happened to his brother—the shooting, the organ-transplant surgery, the ensuing surgeries—those hadn't been his fault. Leaving Alejandro to navigate his teens on his own had.

"He always was amazing." That much was true. Nothing would change that about his brother. All of them were a league above the rest. Him anyway.

"Santiago!"

Saoirse's voice cut through the rage of memories. "We need to load up and roll with this one!"

A smile teased at the corners of his lips. Would he ever get tired of hearing Saoirse's Irish lilt play with American slang?

Probably not, but this is a two-year deal, bro. Man up.

Santiago gave the detective a clap on the arm and grabbed the request for help like the lifeline it was. This was the last place he wanted to revisit the sins of his past.

"Good to see you." It was a lie that would fly.

"You, too, Santi." The detective turned back to the crash site then stopped. "You know we got them, right? Still locked away, as far as I know."

He didn't need to ask who.

"Good." He nodded curtly, unable to open that particular door.

"Valentino! Get yer bony Heliconian ass in gear!"

"Yup!" He kicked up his long-legged stride into a jog. "On my way."

"You okay?" Santi threw Saoirse a cold soda.

"Yeah, why?" She cracked open the can and took a long drink then wiped off her bubbly orange mustache with the satisfied bravura of a six-year-old.

"It's normal to be tired and emotional after ten hours at an accident scene. Especially one like that." He leaned against the sink, taking up his usual pose across the breakfast island from her. Putting a literal barrier between them helped check his body's constant impulse to touch her. A little.

"Ha! As if. It felt…" Saoirse fished around for the perfect word. "I obviously would've preferred no one got hurt, but the way we worked today? It felt *empowering*." She emphasized the final word with real feeling, before giving him a sly smile. "Besides, us Irish never get tired and emotional. We're all about the stiff upper lip."

Saoirse tried to crush her soda can the way Santi always did…palm on top…and yelped when her effort failed spectacularly.

"C'mon. Hand it over." Santi gave a fake sigh of exasperation, all the while making a give-it-here gesture with his hand. When she failed to give it up, he smashed the can, basketballed it into the recycling then took her hand in his, feeling at once at peace and complete.

"Ouch! Don't poke it so hard." She yanked it out of his hand.

"So much for your stiff upper lip." He snickered, grabbing an ice pack from the freezer and curled her fingers gently around it. "I thought that was for the British, anyway, and y'all were the whimsical, emotive types."

She gave him a heavy-lidded look, as if weary of his overtly North American understanding of things.

"I'm not above stealing another country's trait if it suits me," she intoned with a sage nod, stealing a slurp of his own, unfinished soda. "And since when do you say 'y'all'?"

"Since forever. I save it for special occasions."

"This is special?"

"Absolutely."

When their eyes connected, Santi knew instantly he hadn't been hallucinating the electric charges passing between the two of them ever since they'd kissed.

"You're not talking about words anymore, are you?" Saoirse's voice was barely a whisper.

A counter's width was suddenly too great a distance from her. Before he could think better of it—think of anything at all—Santi rounded the breakfast bar and had her in his arms, his mouth seeking answers to the questions that had been all but eating him alive since he'd moved in with her.

The heat and passion with which she met his fierce kisses were all the answer he needed. He scooped her up from her go-to perch on the kitchen stool and carried her into her bedroom—

a room he had been strictly forbidden to enter. He wasn't hearing a hint of a protest now…just a mumbled half thought about minding her hand.

"Don't you worry, *querida*. I will never hurt you."

Saoirse stiffened in his arms, pushing him back to arm's length. "How can you say that? How can you make a promise like that?"

His gaze traveled from her pure blue eyes to her cheeks, flushed with the day's sun and the moment's emotion…her mouth. Her heaven-sent mouth that never needed an ounce of lipstick or gloss to make it shine the deep red it was now.

Because I love you.

Those were the words he ached to say. The risk he felt he couldn't take.

"I made a promise."

"To keep me legal, not to offer a life of wedded bliss." Saoirse's eyes were glued to his as if searching his very soul for any sign he would disappoint her. It was then he knew, without question, how much he loved her.

This moment—giving herself freely to another man—was a hurdle she'd not yet crossed after her idiot of an ex had betrayed her.

He swore softly under his breath. Santi couldn't even imagine—didn't *want* to imagine—the sort of man who would do that to a woman. More particularly the wiggly woman he was just barely managing to hold in his arms.

"Are you having some sort of internal battle?" She pressed her hands against his chest and fully extricated herself from his arms. "I can't do this, Santi. Not if you don't—"

She stopped in midflow, her lips still parted as if she were on the brink of making the same confession he wanted to. Opening her heart to the possibility of love.

Just as quickly she regrouped, grabbed his shirt and tugged him to her as if her very life depended on it.

When their lips met and bodies collided, Santi was virtually consumed by desire. He wanted each moment to be special for her. Cherished. Meaningful.

He forced himself to take things slowly...*lovingly*.

He might not be able to say the words that mattered most just yet. *Por Dios!* He felt them to his very marrow. Through the dappled light of the afternoon sun, their bodies moved in a synchronicity he only would have believed possible with a soul mate. Was this what true love was? Knowing, anticipating, finding just the right spot to stroke and caress her to elicit pleasure-filled moans? When they were physically as one, he could no longer hold back, whispering again and again as their bodies reached an unparalleled release in unison, *"Te adoro. Te adoro."*

"There's absolutely nothing in here we can eat and I'm starving," Saorise wailed.

Having…*relations*…with Santi had ramped up her rumbling stomach to earthquake level.

Santi gave her booty a little bump, his thigh still deliciously bare of clothing, before draping his arm along the length of the refrigerator door.

For the love of St. Patrick and all his blessed leprechauns. Santiago Valentino floated her boat. If she'd had an entire armada he would float that, too. Having sex with him sounded just crude compared to what they'd just shared. If her heart wasn't the beat-up bruised thing it was, she could almost, without laughing, call what had just happened between the two of them making love. A turn of phrase she'd thought, until now, best confined to soap operas.

"How about a ketchup and mayonnaise sandwich?" Santi smiled up at her, the glow of the refrigerator highlighting the outline of his lips. Lips now… Oh, there it was, the tooth along the lip thing that never failed to… Yup, there went her tummy, doing a giddy, swirly flip.

The uncharacteristic explosion of undiluted happiness was, officially now, a medical term in her book. *The giddy, swirly flip.* Who knew a man could come with a new vocabulary attached to him! She swallowed down her I'm-so-happy giggles and forced herself to focus.

"Mayonnaise and ketchup, you say? Well, normally I would agree that 'twould be a grand combination but we don't have any bread."

"Don't you ever go shopping?"

"I'm not one to cast aspersions, but I do recall a certain someone moving in a week ago and all but eating me out of house and home."

"Liar. There wasn't any food here to eat when I moved in! I'll tell you what I'm hungry for." Santi popped the refrigerator door shut with his foot and tugged Saoirse's fresh-from-the-shower body up against his. She drew swirls along the expanse of his chest with her index finger as she feigned considering whether or not to christen the kitchen while they were at it. They'd only done it twice. Once in the bedroom, a second time in the shower...third time even luckier?

"Have you ever had a Helibana?"

"What? Those sandwiches on the specials board down at Mad Ron's?" She shook her head, just an itsy-bitsy disappointed that he hadn't been hungry to ravish her. As if on cue, he dropped his lips to hers and drew from her a deeply fortifying kiss, their bodies connecting with erotic intent.

Okay...that would do. For now.

"Helibanas," Santi said with a sigh when they finally managed to break away from one

another. "My brothers and I used to eat them by the dozen."

"I've seen two of your brothers." Saoirse laughed softly at Santi's faraway gaze. Food, it seemed, was his gateway to memory lane. "If your little brother is anything like the other two, I believe it. Do Valentinos only come in tall or extra tall?"

He didn't answer and she watched as his eyes flicked up to the clock. Eight o'clock on Sunday night. She could practically see his mind zipping through a reel of decision making, his lips opening to begin a sentence, reconsider, then open again to start another. It *had* been a long day and as much as she'd like to jump back into bed, the man needed to be fed and watered.

"Santi, shall I put you out of your misery and drive down to Mad Ron's and get you one of your cherished sandwiches?"

His grin widened. "Let's both go. One definitely won't be enough."

He gave her cheek a noisy kiss and virtually bounded back to the bedroom, where their clothes had been dispensed with in ridiculously hasty fashion. Funny, she thought as she rounded the breakfast bar to follow him. This was the first time she'd wandered around her home—here or in Ireland—absolutely starkers and felt…beautiful. Her gaze shifted along to the bedroom door where she could hear jeans being tugged on and a song being half sung, half hummed. Was humming in Spanish even a thing?

She looked down at her body, the body she'd grown to despise over the last year, and gave it a grin. She felt good. She felt happy. About all of this. Nothing she wanted to put a name to. Not when it made her feel so click-her-heels-together gleeful. Maybe she'd hit the perfect combo. Great job, great city, gorgeous…whatever he was. Fake-fiancé with benefits?

This time around? No labels. Everything had been all but prescribed in her old life—and now? Santiago was single-handedly doing more than any vitamin or visit to the spa with a girlfriend could. For her heart, for her soul, for the giddy, swirly loop-the-loops her stomach had never done before…

What was it Santi always said?

Córcholis!

Goodness gracious, indeed. The man was all the medicine she needed. So…she scribbled a mental prescription to herself: No analyzing, no getting too, too close… What they had was perfect. Like it or not, it was go-with-the-flow-o'clock. Or—she grinned when Santi strode out of the bedroom, throwing her a sundress as he did—in tonight's case, it was Mad Ron's o'clock.

CHAPTER EIGHT

"I'M SURPRISED YOU don't have shares in this place, Santi."

"We probably do."

"We?" Saoirse kept her tone light, but Santi could tell she knew the answer before she asked it. Even he noticed he was mentioning his brothers more frequently. His tone was less defensive each time, as though Saoirse was his safe harbor for all the complicated issues he was trying to unravel. He stole a piece of fried plantain and confirmed what she already knew. "Me and my brothers. We practically used to live here."

"And why not? There's everything a growing boy needs. Helibanas and endless refills of iced tea." Saoirse snickered, all the while squeezing lime juice onto her ever-diminishing pile of fried plantains. "You won't have worried about scurvy anyhow."

"Yes." Santi nodded gravely. "That's why we came here. To ward off scurvy."

"Stop it!" Saoirse giggled, slapping away Santi's hand as he tried, for the umpteenth time, to tug the pickles out of her toasted sandwich.

"They're the best part!" he protested, as if it was his earthly right to possess all her dill pickles.

"Precisely," she retorted, extracting a sliver of pickle from amid the melty goo of cheese, pork and onion and popping it into her mouth. "Which is why *I* want to eat it."

"You'd think you were pregnant the way you're relishing that thing."

The instant he'd said it he wished the moment away.

Up until he'd opened his big mouth, Saoirse had actually been glowing with something better than happiness—*contentment*. And the fact that he'd had even the tiniest bit to do with that had put a satisfied smile on his lips, too.

"Don't. Just…" He tried to wave away his words. "Don't listen to a thing that comes out of my mouth. Unless, of course, it's wise and quotable."

She gave him a dubious sidelong glance then took another big munch of pickle. "And what was it that made you think I ever bothered listening to a word you said, sensible or otherwise?"

And there it was—the smile that lit up his world—back on show in his favorite corner of his favorite cantina in the best city in the world. If only…

The hole in his life that had yet to be filled yawned wider.

It was time.

He needed to set things straight with his brothers. He'd spent weeks *dithering*, if he was being really honest, and waiting for the best moment if he wasn't. With so much that was coming good in his life, he needed to stop stalling.

He waved a hand at the waitress, signaling their need for another round. *Maybe just a bit more stalling...fortifying himself would be essential.*

"Not for me," Saoirse protested, plopping her hands on her belly as if to prove her point. "Two was more than enough. Anymore and everyone will think I look preg—"

She stopped in midflow, a film of tears clouding her tropical blue eyes before she could look away and scrub them clean. She pulled her fists away from her eyes and glared. "See what you've done? Now I've got pregnancy on my mind." It was impossible not to notice the quiver in her normally steady voice.

"Hey," he said softly, pressing a hand atop hers and stroking the back of his other hand along her cheek. "Believe me, Murph. Your belly is just perfect." And it was. Everything about her was exactly right. Beautiful. "And just think!" He scrambled for a bright side. "No stretch marks. Ever!"

If you couldn't dig deep enough to heal the wound, crack a joke. It was how he'd survived. Saoirse deserved more, but it was what he had on offer. A fake marriage. Bad jokes. Unzipping his heart and showing her what he really felt? Not there yet. Not by a long shot.

She pursed her lips at him and grabbed her iced tea, giving the oversize glass a sharp jiggle before she put her beautifully pouty lips around the straw.

Mio Dios, she could rule an army of thousands if she dared.

He wove his fingers together, inverted and stretched them, his bare ring finger standing out among the weave of digits. He'd promised to make an honest woman of Saoirse. As if she needed validating. Or more honesty.

She was more painfully honest than most. Painful only in that she confronted the truth head on. Boldly. Courageously. Life had treated her cruelly and she had come back fighting. She was an inspiration to him. And endlessly cheeky, he realized when he caught her loading her straw with ice water and flicking it at him.

"What's that for?"

"The false optimism! Besides, if you had it your way and I kept eating these sandwiches by the bushel load?" She blew out her cheeks then deflated them with a pop. "You'd have a lot more on your hands than you ever bargained for."

"*Chamaquita*, in my culture a few more pounds on that skinny little frame of yours would be nothing to worry about. If I took you home to my mother…"

Now it was his turn to look away. What a pair they were!

Yes, it had been a long day. Even longer for Saoirse, who'd risen at dawn to do her rounds on the racetrack, but what was all this getting-misty-eyed business? He'd long ago committed his tear ducts to an unbreakable pact. They didn't work. Ever. And in exchange? He would do little to nothing to fight it. So why were they playing up now? Little doubt it had something to do with the woman slipping her hand onto his thigh and giving his leg a gentle squeeze.

"Why don't you go?" The compassion in Saoirse's voice almost tipped the balance.

"*Qué?*"

"To your brothers. It's written all over your face. And they're the closest link you have to your mother, so…short of us hunting down someone who can do a séance…"

His eyes widened.

"One Helibana with extra sauce." He barely heard the waitress as she slipped the sandwich onto the table, his hunger vanishing simultaneously.

"We'll have that to go, please." Saoirse smiled gently up at the waitress then stopped her with a quick "Ah!" before she left. "Would it be all right to make that about eight sandwiches to go?"

"Eight?" The waitress's disbelief was nearly as deep-seated as Santi's.

"No. You're right. Make that a dozen." Saoirse pointed generically toward the door then leaned in conspiratorially, "Valentino stocktaking night."

The waitress nodded, smiling with a hit of recognition, then swished away.

"Well, look who's all proud of herself for hitting the nail on the head," Santi said to cover the surge of emotion filling up his chest like a lead balloon.

"Santi? Do you think I was born yesterday or something?"

"No, but I—"

"I saw your face when you were talking to that copper before."

"The detective?"

"The badge-wearing guy, yeah. You looked like you'd seen a ghost and then you got all intense and broody for the next couple of hours. Not to mention the fact you've only mentioned stocktaking night about four hundred thousand times in the ambulance."

"Have I?" his eyebrows shot up. "I don't get brood—"

She cut him off with a cluck of her tongue. "Don't even bother. You're just lucky I took pity on you and made sweet love to you all afternoon to keep your mind off your troubles." She sat back with a satisfied grin, all the while rat-a-tat-tatting her I-know-I'm-right fingers along the edge of the wooden tabletop.

"First of all, young lady, I think you'll find it was me who made the first move." Santiago drew himself up to what he hoped was his most impressive height.

"First of all nothing." Saoirse shook her head with a quick no-you-don't finger wag that would've sent any child running to the naughty corner of their own volition.

Damn. It was a crying shame this woman wouldn't be a mother. Any offspring of hers would be about as well behaved as they came, too terrified to contest the finger wag.

"There's a reason I haven't been to see them yet." Santi felt a muscle in his jaw twitch. Feeble, he knew. But it was his truth and he was going to own it. He wanted to be *ready* to see them.

"In my book? The best time to do something like this is when you're least prepared. That way you're expecting very little…" Saoirse collapsed her spine into a curve then sprang back upright "…and your bounce-back factor will be high."

"My bounce-back factor?"

"Yes. You'll be needing that if things don't go well."

"So you're already banking on failure?" He bristled.

She snorted. "Santiago Valentino, I've never heard such balderdash in all my days. You are the strongest, most capable, failure-free zone of a human I've ever had the honor to work with."

He shook his head. Now wasn't the time for basking in undeserved compliments. "It's not that simple."

"You are, of course, completely free to share and explain why trotting down the road and telling your brothers you're back in town is so difficult, but in *my culture*..." she paused for effect, the hint of a twinkle in her eyes "...we harbor our secrets close to our chests unless the whole village knows about it anyway, in which case there's not much point in discussing what's already a done deal. The point being, I fled for something everyone knew about. There was no need to spell it all out for folk. Public humiliation does that to a girl, but I'm getting the feeling you're the only one who knows why you left."

"I left a note."

"Someone's sounding a bit defensive." She snorted.

"I could have just left! No note—nothing!"

"Really? Is that what you could have done?" Saoirse looked at him as if he'd just told the biggest honking lie of the lot. But she hadn't known him then. Rebel without a cause didn't even begin to cover it. The motorcycle was all that remained of his bad-boy image he'd fine-tuned to teenage perfection.

"You don't know what kind of man—kid—I was back then." He scrubbed his hands through his hair. "I wasn't a big fan of who I was becoming, this restless, confused mess."

"Not so much of a mess you didn't recognize what was happening. And not so much of a mess you didn't man up and do something about it. Besides," she added with a grin, "you did leave a note."

"It wasn't a back-in-five sort of job!" He snapped. "Sorry, I just—"

"Are we feeling a bit touchy because someone is actually going to go and do this thing?"

"Very."

Jangling nerves were getting the better of him and that's not how he wanted this to go. He'd joined the military to gain better control over himself—his emotions, his goals, his future. And here he was, messing it all up again.

Maybe that was the irony. When he'd been on duty in the world's cruelest war zones, the main lesson he'd come away with? You couldn't control life—you could only control how you responded to it. He should have had a reminder tattooed on his forearm: *Be the man you know you can be*.

"Tell me about the note," Saoirse said softly.

"It was…it was sort of like a guide to life from fifteen to eighteen. My area of expertise." He appreciated Saoirse's laugh. To describe it now sounded so juvenile, but that's what he had been. Countless miles from adulthood.

"And what was all this wise advice you were offering your brother?"

"It was reams—well, not exactly reams but it was vital information for a thirteen-year-old. The coolest place to hang out. Which locker bay to get assigned when he was a senior in high school, which streets to steer clear of because of the gangs, although he pretty much knew that already. Never to take Mr. Prunte's science class because the man was a much better baseball coach than he was science teacher." He watched as Saoirse's eyes grew wider and wider. "I wasn't going to leave Alejandro completely hanging."

"What did you do? Tuck it under his pillow?"

Her words, meant to be jokey, struck him like daggers. Reminders that he had been a coward. Leaving home only to try and prove his mettle on an anonymous battlefield where failure wouldn't feel so personal. But it had. Every life lost had sucked his soul a little bit drier, leaving it little more than an arid wasteland. And now he was supposed to just wander over to the bodega with a sack of sandwiches and make everything all right again?

A surge of frustration washed through him.

"What was I supposed to do, Murph? There's no guide for kids whose parents are shot right in front of them. My kid brother almost died. And all he had was me—the poor second to my older brothers who did the best they could in the circumstances. Looking after us, making good on their full-ride scholarships to medical school while keeping the family business running as well. They don't write those kind of guides, *mija*. I did the best I could."

Saoirse stared at him slack-jawed.

"That may have come out a bit more aggressively than I'd intended." It didn't sound like an apology. But it was one. The best he could do, all things considered.

She shook her head, her fingers steepling in front of her lips. Whether it was to keep words in or out he couldn't tell.

Her fingers parted.

"So, what you're really saying is that your brothers are the only ones in the world who would understand?"

He nodded. Maybe it was a simpleton's view, but that's what his heart was telling him. Saoirse could offer compassion and that, of course, was invaluable…but his brothers had *understanding*. They'd lived through what he'd lived through and for the first few years after their parents had died the shared experience had been an insoluble glue.

"Well, then…" she nodded at the huge paper bag the waitress was carrying in their direction "…I guess you'd better get going."

He heard them before he saw them. The unmistakable laughter. The playful mocking. A sharp chiding for a near miss with a catering-sized can of jalapenos, chased up by a call to throw an extra case of pinto beans to "the ugly one."

Egalitarian brother love.

In the Valentino household? They were all "the ugly one."

"Hé!" he called out a few yards away from the back storeroom where they kept their stock.

The banter continued unabated. They obviously hadn't heard him.

Santi repeated the call, too loudly this time, and all the hustle and bustle of stocktaking clattered to an abrupt halt.

His brothers stood as if in an artist's tableau— all caught in the midst of an everyday action— the expressions on their faces unreadable. He held up the unmistakable delivery bag from Mad Ron's.

What exactly do you say to the people you loved most when you'd walked out on them fifteen years earlier?

"Helibanas? They're still hot."

Alejandro stepped out from the shadows of

the doorway, a flat of canned tomatillos in his hands, his expression unreadable.

Flaca loco, they'd called him.

Alejandro wasn't skinny now. He looked tall, athletic...*muscular*. The opposite of everything those idiot gangbangers had reduced him to with their bullets.

"Hé, gordos!" Alejandro flicked his head toward Santi. "The ugly one finally decided to show."

And with that, he threw the flat of tomatillos toward his brother as if it were weightless. "What are you waiting for, bro? Get counting."

CHAPTER NINE

"Hot sauce, please." Saoirse stuck out a hand.

"Someone's getting a taste for Latino spices." Santi laughed, pushing the bottle of fiery hot sauce across the breakfast bar counter.

"I don't know what they put in this stuff, but it's great!" She gleefully applied splash after splash of the green sauce to her enchiladas.

"I know. Our bodega is one of the only places to stock it. We can hardly keep it in stock."

"Listen to you!" Saoirse teased through a mouthful of burn-your-lips-off enchiladas. "'Our bodega.' 'We can hardly keep it in stock.' When am I going to meet these mythical shopkeeping surgeons anyhow?"

Santiago bristled.

"I'm not stopping you from doing anything."

Saoirse pulled away from the counter where they'd been wolfishly attacking their after-shift meals and gave him a wary look. One that said, *Qué paso, hombre?* And what's with the arm's-length business?

He'd felt it.

She'd felt it.

But joining up the two parts of his life that meant the most to him was proving tougher than he'd thought.

"Valentino," she finally began, "of all the people in your life, you can count me as number one cheerleader in the thank heavens Santi's made friends with his brothers' club!"

"And why is that exactly? Enjoying having the place to yourself now that I've got more responsibilities?"

"Whoa!" Saoirse pushed her plate away and looked at him as if he'd sprouted horns. "Who put grumpy sauce on his *chimichurris*?"

"No one!" he bit back, confirming that someone had, in fact, put not only grumpy sauce but defensive sauce and a splash of get-off-my-back sauce into the mix, as well.

She gave him a gentle smile and a look of infinite tenderness he most assuredly didn't deserve. "C'mon, you big macho man. Tell your..." she hesitated for a fraction of a second "...*friend*, Murphy, all about it."

He opened his mouth to reply and found he couldn't. Her choice of words was exactly the problem. Or, more accurately, just the one.

Friend.

Was that how she really saw their—whatever it was?

Sure, it hadn't been a conventional start to a relationship. The order had been all wrong and the proposal hadn't been a proposal, it had been…a *proposition*. But so much had changed in the weeks since she'd come into his life, including the way he saw her.

Much more than a *friend*.

Which was exactly why he didn't want her meeting his brothers yet. She deserved more than being introduced as a green-card fiancée. Much more.

And until he found some way to pull off the jokey veneer he used to keep the mood between them light and tell her how he really felt? That he loved her? He couldn't—*wouldn't*—introduce her to his brothers. She was precious to him. And the last thing he was going to do was give his brothers even the slightest reason to think less of her than she deserved.

"This whole strong, silent type thing is making me nervous, Valentino." She stabbed at her enchiladas, but was rearranging them now rather than eating. "What gives?"

"I thought you hated it when I talked. Last night you shushed me about a zillion times." He forced on his jocular banter voice. It sounded strangled to him, but her shoulders shifted downward. Less nervous hunch and more feisty blonde.

"That's because you were talking through my

show." Saoirse swooped her fork across the top of her enchiladas, gathering up a wealth of cheese and hot sauce as she did. She circled the fork in front of her mouth, forcing his gaze onto the pair of lips he never failed to be mesmerized by. "You should never, ever talk through my show."

"The paramedics show? Your favorite show is what we do for work all day?"

"Uh-huh."

He smiled as she popped the cheesy blob into her mouth, eyes disappearing under her lids as she gave a satisfied groan.

He was usually the reason she made that sound. Who knew he'd be reduced to duking it out with a forkful of *queso blanco* to be Saoirse's favorite thing. Then again, the *queso blanco* probably would've taken her home to meet the family by now.

"I like watching it to reassure myself that I'm better," she said after making the most of her mouthful of cheese. "Work's the reason I get up in the morning!"

Santi nodded, eyes quickly averting to the takeaway menus on the freezer door, the stack of phone books holding up one corner of the secondhand sofa—anywhere but on Saoirse.

He wanted to be the reason she got up in the morning. They worked together. They slept together. And he liked it. For the first time in his life he wanted more. He felt his chest grow thick with emotions he usually never let bang around his rib cage.

He pushed away from the counter, brusquely scraping the remains of his meal into the garbage can. Sure, it was his own fault she didn't know how he felt. Didn't make feeling them any easier.

All he had to do was say the words—those three precious words that could change his life forever—but he just wasn't there yet. If he lost Saoirse... He swore under his breath, slamming the lid to the garbage can down as he did.

"What's got into you?" Saoirse was eyeing him warily.

"Nothing."

"Liar."

Santi put his plate into the dishwasher, closed it with an exasperated huff and looked her square in the eye.

"I don't think we should sleep together anymore."

The bright, cheery expression on Saoirse's face completely disappeared. "Okay."

"That's it? That's all you have to say about it? Okay?"

"You're the one who said it, not me." She grabbed her plate, jumped off her stool and in the process of putting the scraps in the garbage can managed to lose the entire plate. She slammed the lid down, leaving the plate to languish among the debris. "And you're the one who hasn't been using the guest room I very specially made up for you."

"Well, I'll be using it now. Don't worry about that."

"Good." She crossed her arms and glared at him.

"Good." He mirrored her defensive stance.

Great. A standoff.

He smacked his forehead suddenly remembering that Ángel down at Mad Ron's knew about their marriage plans. He'd have to tell him to stay shtum as his brothers were no strangers to the cantina.

"Now what? Forgotten to tell me you've also put in for a request for a change of partners while you're at it?" Saoirse was staring at him with undisguised fury and he didn't blame her. He was making a complete and utter hash of things.

"Murph—"

"Oh, so we're back to Murph now, too, are we? And just when I was going to give you a certificate of approval for being able to pronounce my name." She uncrossed then recrossed her arms, foot tapping rapidly against the wooden floor, hands balled into little fists. "May as well get to the point, Santi, and just spit out what you really want to say—the wedding's off."

"No!"

They both froze at the hoarse passion in his

voice. "No, Saoirse. That's not what I'm saying at all."

"Would you mind, then, please, telling me what the blue blazes is going through that pea-sized brain of yours because I've had just about as much disappointment at the altar as a girl can take. I *will not* be humiliated a second time. Especially if the blasted thing isn't even meant to be real!"

Santi's heart shot out searing rays of pain in his chest. He didn't want to cause her pain. The total opposite, in fact. Every time her face lit up when he appeared from around a corner, or she laughed at one of his ridiculous jokes, she made the world—*his world*—a better place to be. But he needed to restart or reboot or wipe the slate clean or whatever the hell a man did when truth and honesty and love needed to be at the fore of everything he was feeling.

"This isn't coming out the way I meant."

"You think?" Saoirse bit back. "As a breakup conversation it's going pretty well from where I'm standing."

"Saoirse, please. I'm juggling a lot of things right now and I just want to make sure I get all of them right. If you hadn't noticed, the whole feelings thing isn't really my forte."

"I could've told you that for nothing," Saoirse replied, a bit of the anger slipping away from her c'mon-I-dare-you-to-just-say-it stance. "But what's that got to do with, you know…" She flicked her thumb in the direction of her bedroom. "Not good enough for you, am I?"

"That is definitely not the problem, *mija*," Santi replied, suddenly seeing the conversation from her perspective. Another knock back. Another hurdle to leap to turn the tables in her own life.

"What is it then?"

Oh, Dios. Was that a wobble in her voice?

"C'mere, you." Santi opened his arms and gestured for her to come to him.

"I'm not budging or letting you lay your sexy hands on me until you explain what on earth is going on with you."

"I just want to square things with my brothers. And with you…"

Her eyebrows lifted expectantly, emotion shining brightly in her eyes.

"Men can't multitask," he finished pathetically.

"So, let me get this straight. You're saying if you sleep with me, you'll be so busy being bewitched by the wonders of my good self you won't be able to sort out your relationship with your brothers?"

"Precisely." He heaved a sigh of relief, only to catch the unchecked roll of Saoirse's eyes. He'd bought himself a bit more time. Time to set things right. For all of them.

"For the record…" Saoirse crossed to him and gave him a narrow-eyed stare "…men are stupid." She zeroed her pointy finger in on his chest and gave him a much-deserved jab in the solar plexus. "Enjoy the guest room, *muchacho*."

CHAPTER TEN

SAOIRSE CLIMBED OUT of the ambulance feeling like cement was setting in her bloodstream. Another day of pretending. Another day of hiding the fact the very fabric of her well-being was being torn apart the further Santi drifted away from their little cocoon of 24/7 togetherness.

Stocktaking with the brothers. Dinner with the brothers. Stopping in for a chat with the brothers. A nosy around the fancy clinic to see how far they had all come.

If she could just *meet* the blighters she wouldn't care! It was everything Santi had wanted and her heart was soaring for him. With him. But being held at a very obvious distance was taking its toll. Especially with the rapidly approaching courthouse date. This was her future after all.

And his?

Well. He was finally getting what he'd come home for. Closure. Peace. Family.

And the fact she didn't factor into any of it was becoming clearer by the second. It didn't stop her from wanting to fight it, though. Didn't stop her from knowing she'd met The One.

She pulled open the back door of the ambulance and raked around for the cleaning supplies.

"Are you coming back tonight? For dinner?" Saoirse feigned utter disinterest in Santi's answer, but when she didn't even get one she chalked the moment up on her growing list of lovelorn-wife moments. Even she hated the sound of her own voice when she sounded all fake cheery.

When they'd kicked this whole thing off? She'd swept away a mountain's worth of concerns. They'd had fun! They'd had sex! They'd worked together and been brilliant because whenever they'd done anything together it had been better!

Those together moments were dropping like flies.

It was now glaringly obvious that Santi's offer of marriage was just what he'd said: a favor. Something to keep him in Miami until he was drawn back into the bosom of the Valentino clan.

Or…hard chest.

Or…whatever it was four brothers did whenever they made peace.

Eat buckets of Helibanas and leave their fake fiancées in the wake of their happy-families parade?

It was looking that way.

Her whole swooping-heart, pitter-pat, pulse-racing thing was just a problem she'd have to sort out on her lonesome.

She stopped her frantic scrubbing of the ambulance door and turned to face a freshly materialized Santi, who was looking at her curiously. He'd been doing it more and more over the past few weeks.

Weeks racing past so fast she could practically hear them taunting her.

Her visa was painfully close to expiring. The unspoken-of wedding was a looming issue on the horizon, no longer the brightly glowing thing she'd been anticipating.

Work had become her go-to companion. She'd used every excuse in the book to rack up extra shifts. Needing a new race suit, needing a new carburetor. Needing an engine rebuild. Suffice it to say her car was taking a pounding on the racetrack these days.

She turned around to see his eyes still solidly locked on her. Paranoia was beginning to set in. Sure, she'd put on a couple of pounds over the past few weeks but that had been comfort eating. Completely understandable considering the circumstances.

"What are you staring at? Haven't you any work to be getting on with?" She shooed him away, quickly going up on tiptoe, trying to check out her reflection in the ambulance window to see if something was smeared on her face. The day had been a particularly messy one and all she wanted right now was a hot shower. She scrubbed at her face even though she saw nothing, and looked back toward Santi.

He was leaning against the ambulance with his legs crossed as he filled out the mileage log. It shouldn't look as sexy as it did, but the pose never failed to make him look like Mr. January straight through to December.

A hot shower with a certain someone might make scrubbing off the day even more pleasant to look forward to.

"No, sorry." He scuffed his boot against the tarmac and looked back up at her. "Previous plans."

"Oh, cool." She plastered on her I'm-so-happy-to-hear-it smile. "Big night out with your brothers?"

"No, not tonight." His eyes met hers with that electric burst of connection. The one that felt as if he'd hit her with starbursts and moonbeams and anything else romantic the world had on offer.

He threw a coin up into the air, caught it and slapped it down on the back of his hand as if he were playing heads or tails with himself. His face lit up with a huge smile. One so sweet it near enough tore her heart from her chest.

"…and so they said we'd get together for a football game or something."

"Sorry? What was that?" She'd been staring at his mouth and not listening to the words again. "You mean soccer?"

"No, American football, you doofus." He crossed over to the ambulance, threw the clipboard he'd been filling in onto the gurney then crooked his elbow around her neck and gave her one of those goofy knuckle-rubs on her head. The kind you'd give a brother...or a little sister. Two months ago? Perfect. Now? It felt like she was being downgraded.

What a difference a reconciliation with your family could make.

"Ah, Murph, good times, eh? It's been great catching up with them. Like I've become whole again."

She watched as he drifted away to that faraway place she'd seen him revisit again and again over the past few weeks before remembering he was in midconversation. "You'd love them," he tacked on, a shot of panic in his amber-flecked eyes making the Great Unsaid of the whole exchange come through loud and clear.

"All it takes is an invitation!"

Take that, you unwitting heartbreaker.

"Thanks, Miss Manners. Got it." He tapped his head as if storing away a great tip for folding napkins at his next formal dinner party. In other words, straight into the mental garbage can.

She turned away, fighting the painful sting of tears.

She wasn't going to meet them. Not unless she suddenly needed a neurosurgeon, an epidemiologist and a pediatric-transplant surgeon all at once.

And yet?

None of this was sitting right. Santi didn't give panicky glances. He was all male. A macho, muscled-up hombre with a take-no-prisoners smile. He looked like a poster boy for the Marines he had so recently belonged to. Throw away the gun, toss in a stethoscope and boom! Santiago Valentino. She snuck a peek at him, her scrubbing arm coming to a slow halt as she did.

She gave her shoulders a shake and started scrubbing again. Hard.

"So, um…" Santi began with an uncharacteristic absence of speaking skills.

She took a stab in the dark at what he was trying to say. "Catch you later?"

"Yeah, I guess. Maybe we'll grab a bite if I get back in time?" He gave her a weird, halfhearted pat on the back, a distracted peck on the cheek—one you'd give your grandmother—and wandered off, lost in the deepest of thought.

She grabbed hold of the door and sank onto the thick lip of the ambulance's bumper as a sour cramping sensation rushed into her gut so violently she gasped.

He wanted out.

Now that he had his brothers in his life again—brothers he had fastidiously avoided introducing her to—he didn't need to do good deeds anymore.

"Hey, Valentino!" she shouted after his retreating figure, hands pressed to her knees in a facsimile of looking good, feeling good. "Don't worry about dinner. I think I'm going to try and grab another shift. I heard they're short tonight."

"Oh! All right." He nodded as if really taking the news on board and finding it difficult to digest. "Good. Good. See you later, then."

"Santi?" she called out again.

When he turned around the look of hope and expectation on his face all but took her breath away.

Those eyes of his, amber-flecked portals to all the answers of the universe. His beautiful mouth, lips slightly parted as if he were about to ask her a question. That dark hair she'd become addicted to running her fingers through could've done with a bit of a tweak right now. Not that devilishly rakish didn't work for the man. Far from it. She felt a small tremor begin to take hold of her fingers, spreading and gaining traction throughout her body. The sum of this man's parts was now adding up to one terrifying reality: she was in trouble. And in the one way she'd vowed never to get hurt again.

"Drive safe."

It came out as more of a whisper than the cheery goodbye she'd been aiming for.

"Will do." Santi gave her a half wave and, if she wasn't mistaken, a confused shake of the head as he turned and picked up his long-legged stride toward his motorcycle.

The physical ache she felt as she watched him leave threatened to consume her on the spot. Head down, shoulders tightly hunched up toward her ears so that they all but blocked out the roar of Santi's motorcycle being shifted from low to high gear as he swept out of Seaside Hospital's parking lot and off into the glowing remains of the evening light.

An emptiness began to fill her like darkness.

She shook her head again and again. She hadn't traveled this far and worked as hard as she had only to become a victim again.

This time she was in charge of her destiny.

This time she held the reins.

It was worth it. At least it would be. Wearing the emotional flak jacket to stave off Saoirse's death glares and poorly disguised disappointment in him.

He knew he was being protective of her meeting his brothers. But not for the reasons she thought.

The number of times he'd thought of telling

them about her…he just couldn't pick where to begin when they were still working their way around their newfound relationships.

"So…there's this girl I met…"

"Funny thing happened at work the other day."

"What do you get when you put an Irish paramedic and a Heliconian Marine in a courthouse?"

An arranged marriage!

It wasn't funny. And it certainly wasn't a joke.

A tug at his conscience reminded him of the streak of sadness in Saoirse's voice when he'd left tonight.

He'd caused that. And he'd be the one to fix it. Turn her frown upside down.

Dios!

What a dork.

He opened the throttle on his bike just to remind himself of his own virility.

Taking the turn into town instead of off to the Keys was equally satisfying.

He was putting down roots. Building a new future.

All that was left to discover was how big a role Saoirse was going to play in it.

"Hey! Where's the fire?"

"Amanda! Sorry, I didn't see you there." Saoirse's focus had been so intent she'd marched straight past her friend. "You off shift?"

"Yeah, how did you guess?" Her friend gave

her trademark smirk as she retied the bikini neck strings looping over the back of her baggy sweatshirt.

"Meeting James at the beach?"

"And the observational powers prize goes to Saoirse Murphy!"

Saoirse's jaw dropped.

"What? What did I say?" Amanda looked over her shoulder as if the words were still lingering there.

"You got it right."

"What right?"

"My name. It's the first time you've got my name right!"

"Really?" Amanda beamed. "I wasn't even trying! Hooray for me!" She grabbed hold of Saoirse's elbow with both hands and tugged. "Why don't you come along? We'll have a swim, and then we'll ditch James. He's always working at night anyway so we can go to Mad Ron's and drink mojitos."

A wave of nausea lurched across Saoirse's midriff. She'd been giving Mad Ron's a wide berth since "the reunion."

"What's wrong?" Amanda's forehead crinkled. "You love Mad Ron's and we haven't been for ages."

"I know, I was just…" Oh, no. Oh, please… oh, please, no. Tears were stinging at the back of her throat. She held her breath. She swallowed. She held her breath again.

"Oh, Murph! C'mon. I have a good guess where you were heading so let's get there and fast." Amanda steered her around past the main check-in counter and headed toward the elevators, proving she knew her friend well.

"What about James?"

Her voice cracked horribly and the tears she'd been valiantly holding at bay lurched up to balance precariously on the rims of her eyes.

You idiot! Tip your head back. Tip your head back and make them go away.

"I'll send him a text. He never actually wants to go, but I make him because otherwise I don't think he'd ever leave the office. Enforced date night," she added, all the while jabbing the elevator buttons. "All work and no play makes James a dull boy."

Mercifully, the doors opened to an empty elevator and Saoirse felt herself being shuttled in as the film of tears grew thicker and thicker by the moment.

"No!" Amanda put out her hand to stop a family carrying fistfuls of balloons and armfuls of flowers from entering the elevator. "Sorry! Medical emergency, this one's taken."

Saoirse opened her mouth to protest, but in so doing lost her battle with the tears she'd been trying to hold at bay.

"Right!" Amanda tugged a tissue out of her never-ending stash and scrubbed at her friend's face as if she were a toddler. "What's going on?"

"I don't want to talk about it," Saoirse mumble-sniffed.

I'm in love with Santiago and it's never going to happen!

"It's Santiago, isn't it? Are you in love with him?"

"How—"

"It's only been written all over your doe-eyed face for the past few weeks, Murphy."

"You have permission to say my name now." Saoirse tried to smile through her tears and ended up doing a weird hiccup thing instead.

"I'm not going to risk it." Amanda nodded seriously, clearing a path through the crowd waiting outside the third-floor elevator bay. "There's only so much damage control a girl can do. Take a right here."

Saoirse nodded, even though she didn't need directions. This was the first place she'd visited when choosing which hospital she wanted to work for. A visual reminder of where she *didn't* want to find herself in another year's time. But as the familiar sights and sounds of the department began to hit her she wondered if perhaps she hadn't been a bit hasty.

The soft lighting, the hushed tones, deeply cushioned armchairs, monitors everywhere. The whirr and steady cadence of lifesaving equipment all wove together into the core ingredients of the department where she'd begun her medical career.

A complication of emotions started crisscrossing her heart as she pressed her face up against the window of the NICU's main hub—a fan of incubators spread out before her in a room with all the equipment an infant fighting for survival could need. A few more tears rolled down her cheeks before she felt she was ready to turn the handle and enter.

The familiar scents hit her with unexpected strength. It shouldn't have surprised her—scent being one of the most evocative of sensations—but she felt her body being infused with all that she had left behind. She took a deep breath and walked straight into the middle of the room before allowing herself to take it all in. Amanda waited at the doorway of the midsize room, knowing more than Saoirse did herself that alone time with all the tiny babies in NICU was going to be the healing elixir she needed right now.

The details of why each child was there came to her before she read their charts. It had always been a point of pride back in Ireland—the connection she'd instantly shared with the newborn souls fighting for the lives they were meant to lead. A daughter's heart that needed a bit more time to grow. A transfusion for a son who needed a boost of red blood cells. Twins whose blood types were mysteriously incompatible with their mother's, overwhelming their tiny little livers, giving their soft skin a jaundiced taint. All of them united in their efforts to survive.

This world was so familiar to her she probably could have gone through it blindfolded. But then you didn't get the plus side of seeing all the tiny fingers and tiny toes…little rosebud mouths and noses just begging for a kiss to be popped onto them.

A sigh left her as she realized it had only been some nine months ago that she'd thought the last place on earth she'd find comfort was the NICU and yet…in the time it took a baby to gestate…

Was she really back where she'd begun this journey? Heartbroken and alone?

She ran her fingers along the incubator closest to her and had to smile. Another set of twins. Cheek to cheek and holding hands. They couldn't have been more than a kilo each. Fragile and *resilient*. That's what these little ones were. She could sense it in the connection they shared with each other as they slept, their bodies unconsciously doing everything they could to stay alive. The medical teams who cared for them— quietly, and with dogged determination—doing the same.

Tiny oxygen tubes were taped—pink for one,

blue for the other—along their miniature upper lips. She scanned their charts.

RDS. Respiratory distress syndrome often afflicted preemies, landing them in the NICU for C-PAP treatment. The air they received from the thin oxygen tubes helped keep the small air sacs in their lungs from collapsing. It was a good sign that they had the nose tubes. Some of the sickest children needed mechanical ventilators to breathe for them while their lungs strengthened and recovered. Fighters. The lot of them.

Just like she needed to be.

"Happier now?"

Amanda wandered over. As Saoirse looked up, she realized she was mirroring the broad smile on her friend's lips.

"Yes, thanks. I just…" She ran her fingers through her hair with a little "Urgh!" noise. "You're right. About Santiago and the being-in-love thing." She decided on the truth after running through the thousands of denials she could have given. Sure, the truth hurt. But it was better to take it all in one painful hit than prolong the inevitable.

Amanda clapped her hands together gleefully, eyebrows lifted with happy expectation, and just as suddenly furrowed her brow and knitted her fingers together underneath her chin with a snort.

"But that's a good thing, right? Why aren't

those happy tears?" Amanda looked bewildered. "Are you saying he doesn't feel the same way?"

"Yes. I mean no." She tugged two tufts of hair between each set of fingers and began to twist. It was her new go-to thinking-while-doing gesture. "I mean, I love him but I'm pretty sure he doesn't love me."

"Pretty sure or absolutely sure?" Amanda pressed.

"Pretty absolutely?" Saoirse scanned the NICU, mercifully bereft of visiting parents. A couple of nurses were discussing some paperwork in a far corner. Not too many witnesses to her meltdown.

"Ever since Santi's made up with his brothers he's just been... I don't know." She looked up to the ceiling for inspiration and found none.

"Distant?" Amanda tried.

"Yeah." Saoirse nodded. "Something like that. Distant and just not... We had a real connection, you know?" And as the words came out of her mouth the enormity of the loss she was suffering struck her again. Santi wasn't just a hot man who took her to ecstatic heights in the bedroom. He was the real deal. He had depth. Compassion, follow-through... The number of patients they'd dropped off who he went to check up on afterward... She'd long ago lost count. Not everyone was like that. And not everyone was man enough to own up to decisions they'd made and had gone back to change them as he had with his brothers.

"Have you ever thought of coming back?"

"What, to Miami? You mean, once I get deported when this whole marriage sham doesn't work out?"

"No." Amanda pressed her palm down, signaling Saoirse to keep it quiet. And she was right. Of course. Being the center of hospital gossip was the last thing she needed. "I meant, Murph, have you ever considered coming back to NICU?"

"Not really." She'd been so intent on making her life look as different as she could when she'd moved here, a return to a job she had genuinely enjoyed hadn't factored. "Why?"

"Well, there are a couple of reasons. And don't think I'm saying this because I agree with you. You've been working your backside off these past few weeks and, I suspect, burning a bit of the naughty midnight oil with your new housemate, so you're probably just—"

"I am *not* tired and emotional!" she whisper-growled. What was it with these Americans, flinging about their tireds and emotionals like they were going out of style? And so what if she was? There was no point in highlighting the bleedin' obvious, was there?

"All I was going to say, if you could zip it for a minute and listen—" Amanda fixed her in her best shut-your-trap glare "—is that if you came back to NICU, even though I know it would be tough and you'd have to slay some demons, it would give you a bit more breathing space. You and Santi work together all day, then I don't even know what all night. That's a lot of together time."

"You and James are always together!" Saoirse shot back defensively. She hated being the object of scrutiny, particularly with her cherished best friend hitting the nail on the head with every verbal blow.

"No, we're not! I work here. He works at a law firm. Both of us work long hours. And mine are erratic, which means I see him even less. The reason I make him come swimming with me is so we have at least an hour together two or three times a week that isn't filled with me trying to pry him away from the mountains of paperwork he's always reading so we can afford our dream house and have our dream baby if he would ever, for once, not be so tired he falls asleep at the kitchen table. Or on the sofa. Or in the armchair. Am I painting a picture of reality here? Life's not perfect. But you can find a way to make it work if you're willing."

She had a point, but Saoirse had worked herself up into a right old tizzy and that beast needed purging.

"If he's sick of me already, then he's certainly

not going to want to fake marry me and have me mooning all over him until he can file divorce papers." Even saying the words made her stomach surge in protest.

"In which case…" Amanda made a hear-me-out face. "If you transfer to NICU, maybe you could renew your student work visa and sign up for some specialty course? Quit shaking your head. That was the plan in the first place. Maybe in transplants—"

"No way!" Saoirse protested. "Santi's brother does that. I am not going to spend my days with another Valentino if this goes south."

"If," Amanda repeated pointedly. "That's the key word. And I'm pretty sure Alejandro's single—"

Saoirse clapped a hand over her friend's mouth in midflow. "I am *not* participating in another marriage that doesn't happen and another career veer! And I am *definitely* not putting myself in the path of another Valentino. No. Way."

"For goodness' sake, Murphy! Look at the bright side, would you?"

"I'm not really seeing one right now, isn't that obvious?" She swiped at another bonus spill of tears on her cheeks.

Without Santi in her life, it just didn't feel like there could be a bright side. She'd be just as well returning to Ireland and living the life destiny had made for her. Spinsterhood and caring for children she would never have herself...

Santi was a man who would want children. She could see it in his eyes every time he picked up an injured child or sick baby. Just the sight of his large, capable hands cupping the head of an infant... Despite her best efforts, a sob of pure grief left her throat.

She could never give Santi a family of his own—so stealing two years of his life just so she could get a visa would be little short of cruel.

She vaguely saw Amanda zooming in and out of focus as her friend tried to get her attention back from Never, Never Get What You Want Land.

"You've got me as a friend!" Amanda chirped lamely.

Saoirse accepted the hug she was being pulled into, arms hanging limply by her sides. Amanda was right. She had a great friend...and a few weeks left on her current visa. Plenty of time—ish—to sort out something new. But if she was going to make the rest of her life something worth living, she would have to proceed with her dignity and pride intact, which meant there was only one course of action she could take.

Her mind made up, she gave her friend a grim smile. No point in testing the boundaries of Amanda's friendship more than she already had.

"Go find James. I don't want to mess with

swim time." She hooked her arm through Amanda's, a feeling of determination taking hold. "I'll walk you out."

"You sure you're going to be all right?" Worry was strong in her friend's voice. "No going loop-the-loop or drowning your sorrows in a swimming pool of margaritas or anything stupid, right?"

"Absolutely not. I'm feeling better already," Saoirse said solidly, turning their pace into a jaunty hop-skip. Faking it would have to work for now. "After all, we're in Magic City!"

CHAPTER ELEVEN

"SHE'LL LOVE IT."

"It is beautiful…" Santi held the ring up to eye level again.

When it hit the light, the solitaire rose-cut diamond sent a panoply of rainbows playing over the saleswoman's face. She knew her business. That much was clear. She'd cleverly got him describing Saoirse, her petite frame, her take-no-prisoners attitude, her pure blue eyes, pixie-like blond hair… He didn't know if she did this to every male customer who came in but it certainly hadn't been hard work to get him to big up Saoirse.

He narrowed his eyes, blurring everything else out of his vision, so that he could only see the ring.

It *was* beautiful. A rose for his rose. Or the woman he hoped would continue to bloom and blossom if she were to accept his proposal. His very real proposal.

"She's not very…girlie…"

An image of Saoirse in her fireproof racing gear, helmet tucked under her arm, hair a bit wild after a good run sprang into his mind. Maybe he should get a washer from a muscle car engine studded with diamonds instead. "I'm beginning to think the rose gold band might be a bit too princessy?"

"From everything you've said to me, she sounds incredibly feminine," the chic woman replied, then tilted her head, grinning at his indecisiveness. "There isn't a woman I've met—ever—who doesn't have a bit of princess in her. Especially if she's met her Prince Charming!"

Santi barked out a laugh. As if! The last look Saoirse had shot him? Ogre would've been a better call than prince.

Then again, that was kind of the point, wasn't it? He'd never really pictured himself as a white knight riding to her rescue when he said he'd help her out with her visa problems. Volunteering had been a way to keep himself nailed to Miami till he faced up to his past. Selfishness disguised as heroism.

This time around? If she said yes? She'd be the one coming to his rescue because he didn't think he'd be able to stem the hole in his heart if she left.

"I think she'll adore it. And..." she leaned in for added effect "...in my experience, most woman go cuckoo for whatever ring they are given, because it's from the man they love. She loves you? She'll love the ring."

Santi felt his blood pressure rise. This was all getting a bit complicated.

In Man World things were a bit more black and white. Man loved woman. Man bought ring. Man bent knee. Woman said yes, someone gave them a new barbecue at their wedding and they all lived happily ever after.

Or something like that anyway.

Things weren't so simple with Saoirse and him.

He twisted the ring back and forth as if it were a crystal ball.

It wasn't exactly as if the pair of them were skipping along Miami Beach, telling one another how in love they were. Quite the opposite, in fact.

And that was on him. He'd kept her away from his brothers to protect her—but it was pretty easy to see she'd taken it the other way around. As if she weren't good enough to meet them.

It boiled down to him not wanting them to meet her until she knew how he really felt. He didn't want a fake fiancée. Or a fly-by-night love affair. Not with Saoirse.

He wanted all of the stuff that came with a real marriage. The love. The passion. The stupid fights over who'd used the last squeeze of toothpaste. Hell, he'd even learn how to wash her delicates if that's what it took. And he'd introduce her to his brothers. His bighearted, complicated, not entirely issue-free brothers.

Nerves. That's what it was. Nerves playing havoc with the paths that connected his heart and mind.

"So..." The saleswoman's voice swooped down an octave as she retrieved the ring from Santi's fingers. "Shall I wrap this up for you?"

He nodded brusquely, wary of the panic growing within him. He'd waged hand-to-hand combat with men who would've been more than happy to throw him in a common grave and not bat an eyelash. The simple act of buying an engagement ring? Blithering idiot would've described him nicely.

"Don't worry." The saleswoman gave his hand a soothing pat. "We've had men faint in here before. Panic attacks. One even thought he was having a heart attack, but thankfully the paramedics talked him down and he's now been happily married for the past five years!"

"That obvious, eh?"

Wouldn't that just be the bee's knees? Having a heart attack right here in the ring store and Saoirse showing up as the EMT...

On the other hand, it would be a novel way to propose.

He shook the idea away. Saoirse didn't like public displays of anything. She was a private woman who played her cards close to her chest. He only hoped she was saving her hand for him and not just the visa. If he'd gotten this wrong... No. He wasn't going to go there.

"I've been doing this for a while," the woman replied with a smile as she tucked the sparkling ring into the velvet lining of the eggshell-blue box. "Now, most of our customers wait until their fiancée can join them to pick the actual wedding bands. Would you like to do the same?"

He nodded. Speech, it appeared, was not his partner in crime today.

The rest of the transaction passed relatively pain-free. A life in the forces meant he'd been able to put a fair bit of money away. Money he'd now like to use to buy them a house. Maybe even the little beach house Saoirse was renting if the owner was willing to sell. It wasn't huge, but it was more than big enough for the two of them.

He scanned the countertop ads as the saleswoman organized a little bag for the little box which had to—for some mysterious reason—be enclosed in a sleeve kind of thing. His eyes skidded to a halt when they hit on a ring he hadn't seen before. Two intertwined bands with a weave of inlaid diamonds. It was beautiful.

"Miss—um—I'm sorry. Is it all right if I have a look at this one first?"

Her eyes lit up. "Oh! This is one of our most popular eternity rings. Is your bride-to-be an expectant mother?"

"Why would you ask that?" His eyes zapped to hers.

"Traditionally," she explained, without managing to sound patronizing or hurt that he'd been so brusque, "these rings are bought by a proud father for a new mother. Of course, it is a beautiful ring. If you prefer this to the rose cut, we can change it."

"No." He cut her off sharply. More sharply than he'd intended. The last thing he was going to do was rub it into Saoirse's face that she couldn't have children. The instinctual need to protect her, care for her, were all the push he needed. It was time to do this thing.

"We're good. Go with the gut, right?" He pointed at the little bag she was just tying a ribbon onto. "First choice is the best choice, right?"

"Absolutely," she agreed with a smile. "She'll just love it."

"Thank you," he said, accepting the small bag and undoing all her handiwork by stuffing it into the inside pocket of his leather jacket. "You chose professions well."

"Who wouldn't love being the 'gatekeeper' at the beginning of every couple's journey?"

Her own wedding band and warm smile told him everything he needed to know. She saw marriage as a place of happiness, contentment... being whole. All the things he'd been fruitlessly seeking throughout his military career only to find them back here at home with his family. The family he hoped to expand by one cherished Irish lass.

As he left, Santi held open the door for another man who was looking considerably undecided about entering the store. "Go on," he said with a smile. "I have it on good authority that it's worth it."

"Easy, tiger!"

Saoirse saw her driving instructor's knuckles going white as she hit an S-curve after a chicane with fearless intent.

"I hope this isn't how you drive your ambulance," he gasped.

"It is if I know it will save someone's life," Saoirse replied spikily.

After she and Amanda had said their goodbyes she'd snuck back up to the NICU and then the maternity wards to revisit her options. The sea of babies, all busy doing their own thing—laughing, struggling, triumphing or just plain old sleeping—had reopened wounds she'd foolishly thought she'd laid to rest.

For the first time in…was it months?…she'd thought of her ex. They had never really talked about having children—it had just been an unspoken given. As had so many things. Socking away money in their individual accounts for the house they'd eventually buy. For the school fees they'd one day struggle to cover but wouldn't begrudge because they were for their children's future.

But there hadn't been any *talking* about it. Dreamy-eyed curiosity over whether their children would have his eyes or hers. His common sense and her stick-to-it-iveness.

Come to think of it, they'd never really daydreamed about anything beyond their job opportunities in America. All the rest of the time they'd blindly followed the well-worn path of their friends and family before them. First came love…

But had it? Had it *really*?

It was hard to say now. Tom had been more of a given than a chosen. And when he'd left her there, the priest looking at her as if she'd be able to explain what had just happened, it had been difficult to pinpoint exactly what it was that had ultimately broken her heart and sent her on this journey.

What if her ex had left her because, as Santi

had suggested, he just hadn't wanted to be with her and had used her infertility as an excuse? It's not as if they'd met up at the pub afterward and had a jolly debrief of the whole affair over a pint and a lump of stale wedding cake.

The only godsend had been their separate finances. What if they'd bought a house together? She shuddered at how complicated it would've been to extricate herself from Ireland.

She jammed on the brakes and screeched the Murph-mobile to a halt.

"That was…" Her driving instructor struggled for words. "That was proof someone's been putting in a lot of track time."

"Yeah, well, I think I'll be selling up shortly so I want to make the most of things."

"What? You've only just arrived in the States, haven't you?"

"I've been here long enough." *Long enough to fall in love.*

"Huh." He shook his head as if the words weren't registering. "I thought you'd settle down here in Miami for sure. You seemed to take to it like a duck to water."

Saoirse's fingers clumsily fumbled to unclip her five-point harness as she suddenly needed to gulp some fresh air. Whether it was the gas fumes or the questions that were making her queasy…

"Murph? You all right?"

She unclicked the door as swiftly as she could, unable to hold back the sour swell of nausea any longer.

She could only just hear the unbuckling of harnesses and the passenger door opening and slamming shut through the buzzing in her ears.

"Here you are, honey." Her sixty-something driver instructor, Hal, appeared beside her and handed her a fresh handkerchief. "You just stay put. I'll go and get you some ice water and a cool cloth. You took that course like a bat outta Hades—so I'm not surprised you're a bit queasy."

She nodded dumbly, deep exhaustion coming over her as the nausea ebbed away. When Hal returned, she gratefully accepted the drink. Elbows propped on knees, she kept her eyes on the ground, taking tiny sips of the water for fear she'd be unwell again if she gulped it down.

"Now..." She saw Hal's race-booted feet rock back on his heels. "You've not been doing anything ridiculous like driving while pregnant, have you? I mean the roll bars and safety harnesses will take good care of you but there are a whole passel of other considerations..."

Saoirse stopped hearing Hal's list of safety precautions. She just kept shaking her head...but not as an answer to any of the questions coming her way.

She couldn't be pregnant. She'd been told it was impossible. By a doctor. A specialist even!

Then again, doctors were known to make mistakes.

She *had* felt exhausted lately. It came in hardhitting thwacks of fatigue and then would disappear. And this wasn't the first time she'd been sick. She'd blamed dodgy fish tacos the first time. And what had it been last week? Too much coffee on an empty stomach.

Her stomach roiled in protest as she took in slurp after slurp of water as if the liquid could drown out the voices in her head.

"I think I'm going to take the Murph-mobile home now." She gave the car a pat, pulled her legs back into the driving well and was about to give Hal back his handkerchief.

"Don't worry." He waved away the offer. "I've got dozens of the things. My wife thinks they keep me classy."

Saoirse squinted up at Hal. He'd been married over forty years, if memory served. Potbellied and happy every single day of them, too. The kind of happiness she would very likely never know.

She pulled her door shut, her features caught in the cross fire of a battle to arc her lips into a smile or a grimace. Thankfully the smile won out and she waved her thanks to Hal as she slowly steered her car to the parking bays.

Pregnant?

She didn't want to afford herself a glimmer of hope. Not now. Not before she'd taken a test.

But…if it were true?

A wash of joy filled her body at the thought. *A baby!*

All the little pieces of the puzzle she hadn't realized she was a part of began to fall into place.

It wasn't the future she'd thought she'd have, but it would be a good one.

Santi paced outside Saoirse's bedroom door. Silently, he hoped. He'd already been here ten minutes. Ten *fruitless* minutes working up the courage to knock, let alone ask her to marry him. For real this time. And he didn't want to mess it up. So wasting time as the sunset-proposal window was quickly slipping away wasn't really working.

He'd even sucked up some courage and shown the ring to Alejandro. The punch on his arm had told him everything he'd been hoping for.

Go for it, bro.

Pace. Pace. Pace.

He really should've eased her into their lives before now. He could see he'd messed up on that front. But he was climbing one helluva steep learning curve and the altitude was clearly getting to him.

What was it Saoirse had said when he'd been hedging about with seeing his brothers all those weeks ago?

The best time to do something like this is when you're least prepared.

He wasn't prepared. His heart was thumping in his throat. His chest felt like some sort of bongo jamboree was lurching around in there—barely allowing enough oxygen for him to breathe. Even his fingers weren't playing ball. Every time he'd practiced pulling that little box out of his pocket, they'd shaken.

But more than anything he also knew he was not prepared to lose her and the last two days she'd had a look in her eyes that scared him. The same two days he'd been carrying the ring around in his pocket.

He watched his knuckles give her door a light rap as if they were attached to someone else.

"What do you want?"

"A walk?"

"You're not asking for my permission to take a walk, are you?" She pulled the door open a crack and looked at him through slightly bleary eyes. "Your life is your own, and the beach is public. Please...be my guest."

"I thought we could go together." He stuck his

foot in the doorway, not entirely convinced she wouldn't shut it in his face given half a chance.

"What for?"

"The delights of Miami?" Nice one. Why not apply for a job at the city tourist board when she boots you out of your ambo?

"C'mon, Murph. I'll get you a chocolate-covered frozen banana. You've been eating those things like they've been going out of style the past week."

"So what if I have?" she snapped defensively, her eyes flicking across his face, scanning his features for information.

"C'mon." He held out his hand. If for better or for worse was going to start right now, so be it. "Let's go for a walk. It's a lovely night."

"Fine," she huffed. "I'll just go and grab a jumper. See you on the beach."

The second he moved his foot she slammed the bedroom door shut. Not quite the romantic beginning he'd been hoping for, but expecting the unexpected seemed to be how things were with Saoirse. And for a lifetime of that ride? He could take just about anything.

Saoirse heard the French doors open and close as she yanked a light sweater off a hanger and tugged it on. Good. She needed a few moments to gather her courage for what she needed to tell Santi.

Those websites weren't wrong about raging hormones. Locking herself in her room seemed the only way to keep those monkeys under control.

A baby.

The store-bought test hadn't lied. And the trip to the obstetrics ward after that had been a second confirmation. But the one that had really hit her? The moment where she'd really believed it was true? Yesterday morning. She'd taken some stolen moments in the maternity ward and had sobbed with joy at the sight of all the little creatures wrapped in cottony-soft swaddling.

How on earth could she say it? Or should she say it at all? Leaving Santi none the wiser might be the kindest move, all things considered. He had his brothers now and whatever it was they had…that familial bond…it eclipsed whatever she'd thought the two of them had shared.

She scrubbed her fingers through her hair. It was easiest to rip the bandage straight off, wasn't it? She yanked open the door that led to the beach and faced her future. It was bandage-ripping time.

The setting sun lit Santi up like a film star. Not that he needed any enhancement. He was absolutely perfect. In every way. A truer friend and superlative lover, no matter how fleeting it had been, she thought she would never meet again.

Saoirse felt her heart constrict. It was cruel that loving someone sometimes meant you had to let them go.

Her hands moved to her belly, already aware of the precious life that lay within her. The life she'd vowed to protect, cherish and bring into this world unscathed by any mistakes she'd made in her past. And there had been plenty.

"Hey, you!" Santi turned, his eyes brightening when they connected with her own. A jag of indecision constricted her breath. Was she doing the right thing? She looked into his dark eyes, the flecks of gold appearing virtually molten amid the reflections of orange and red in the sunset.

She swallowed. She wasn't just doing this for herself. Protecting her heart from the pain that would inevitably come her way if she let this whole visa charade go ahead was just part of it.

"I have something I'd like to talk to you about." Santi reached his hand out toward her again. Her arms remained glued to her sides. She couldn't take it. Not with what she was about to do.

"Me first!" It came out much sharper than she'd intended.

Her words acted as a repellent. The sting of hurt she felt when he took a few steps back from her would stay with her forever. All of this would. But she had to do it for her unborn child.

Their surroundings began hitting her in disjointed shards of discord. An elderly couple sharing a picnic beneath a cluster of palm trees. Younger couples watching their children frolicking in the sea, holding up towels as their shivering little bodies emerged squealing from another wash of waves on the shore. The scene sang of joy and harmony. Things every family deserved. Things Santi deserved. Not some fake marriage he'd agreed to when life had been different for him.

"I don't want to go through with it," she finally blurted. "The wedding," she added, as if it weren't blatantly obvious.

Santiago stood statue still for a moment as he registered what she was saying. She saw the tiniest tremor at the edges of his eyes as he narrowed them, assessing her with the cool stillness of a sniper about to take the lethal shot.

"Any particular reason?"

She'd never heard him sound the way he did now. Cold. Unfeeling. The Santi she'd known had been the polar opposite. But what had she expected? That he'd kick his heels up and shout for joy after all he'd done for her? It wasn't just everyone who'd agree to sacrifice two years of their life for someone they'd only just met.

"You said it before. Your brothers—"

"What about them?" His normally sensual mouth was curled in disgust.

"They're your priority. Rightly so," she added, meaning it. "I think I'd be better off doing this whole thing with someone—"

"Who didn't matter?" he finished for her. "Or someone who mattered more?" Santi snarled.

"No! No. It's nothing like that."

"Your ex hasn't swanned back into the picture, has he? Is that what's happened? I thought you had enough gray matter in that brain of yours not to make the same ridiculous mistake twice."

Saoirse stumbled back a step, feeling his words as physical blows. She knew they had become good friends over the past few weeks, but there was force in his words. As if he was…jealous?

No. It wasn't that.

Too much emotion was clouding her judgment. Until this very moment she had been certain his feelings for her hadn't developed in the same way hers had. That he hadn't fallen as head over heels in love as she had.

Why else would he have kiboshed their physical relationship when things had finally come good with his brothers? Why else would he have kept her so far away from the people he loved most? You shared those things! You wove them together. And he'd made it very, very clear she wasn't a part of that.

The last thing she was going to do was trap him with a baby he'd been promised he'd never have, as well.

She dug her heels in the sand, as if it would help strengthen her resolve that she'd chosen the right course of action. If he didn't even want her around while he was with his brothers, he wouldn't want her and the baby.

Their baby.

She crossed her hands over her belly as she forced herself to meet Santi's laser-sharp gaze. "This is my decision. It has nothing to do with anyone else."

"You mean anyone else besides me."

And our baby.

Tears stung at her eyes. "It's not like that, Santi—" she protested.

"You know, *Murphy*," he cut in, waving away her efforts to improve the situation. "I knew all along agreeing to help you was a crazy decision. *Totalemente loco!*" He twirled his index finger next to his temple for her benefit, but he'd been the crazy one. An idiot convinced he could have it all.

She just stared at him, arms crossed over her

body as if it would deflect his reaction to her rejection.

"Well, good for you. You've gone and proved me right. Just as you have made it spectacularly clear that I was wise not to introduce you to my brothers. They value *loyalty*. And commitment. You obviously don't have either trait."

He was lashing out. He knew it. And he couldn't stop.

How could he have misread so badly what had been happening between the pair of them? There might be tears shimmering in those beautiful eyes of hers, but they were obviously a mask for a heart of stone. "Would you be so kind as to afford me a final favor, *mi amor*?"

She nodded dumbly, swiping away a couple of tears as she did. *Why the hell was she doing this if it was hurting her as much as it was hurting him?*

"Stay out here for twenty minutes while I get my things."

"You don't have to move out."

He was unsurprised to hear the bitterness in his humorless laugh. "You think it's a good idea, do you? For me to stay in the 'marital home' while you go about your life? Watch you blindly feel your way around the kitchen every morning until you get your first cup of coffee? Help you with your daily search for the flip-flops you kicked off carelessly the night before? Stand by while you shut yourself away in your bedroom, doing goodness knows what? Or do you feel liberated from your past now that you've had your little rebound?"

He saw the color drain from her face. "This wasn't a rebound at all, Santi. Please. Don't for a moment think—"

"Save it, Murph. You told me from the start this whole thing was a charade. I guess I just played my part a bit too realistically, huh?"

She tried to interject again but he didn't want to hear it. What good would further explanation do other than lacerate his heart completely beyond repair?

He felt the side of him resurface he'd thought he'd left on the battlefields of the Middle East. The hollow, aching, side. The side that could hardly breathe. The side that knew life hadn't finished playing its cruel tricks on him.

Well, this was enough.

He'd had enough.

Saoirse stared with wide-eyed disbelief and he didn't blame her. He was feeling this to the bone, his whole being literally shaking with emotion. A sensation he'd never experienced before.

But the person standing in front of him, rubbing her hands along the spray of goose bumps on her arms, wasn't just any someone. Any woman. She was the woman he loved. He should be pulling her into his arms, keeping her warm, *caring* for her. *Fighting* for her.

Something was off—really off—about the whole thing, but he couldn't abide by this type of about-face.

He raised a hand when her lips parted. "I'll stay at the bodega. There's a room above the shop."

"Santi, please."

"*Cállese!* No. No, you don't." Santi raised his shaking hands and took another step back. "You don't get to look all pitying and tearful. You could have had everything you wanted. This is on you, *cariño*. This is all on you."

It took all of the strength he had not to grab the ring box from his pocket and fling it directly into the sea as he turned away from her.

He would find a way to get through this. He had his brothers now. He was no longer alone. But never before had he felt so abandoned.

CHAPTER TWELVE

HEARTBROKEN DIDN'T EVEN begin to cover the ache of loss Saoirse was feeling. And calling in sick two days in a row was going to compromise what little time she did have left before the bureaucracy of life took over.

The look of utter disbelief...and then disdain that had filled Santi's eyes as he'd absorbed what she'd been saying had savaged any logic she'd thought existed in her plan.

He hadn't just seemed angry because she'd wasted his time. He had seemed *hurt*. As if she were the only one who had treated their "romance" with dismissive whimsy. She felt sick as she began to take on just how low his opinion must be of her now.

Subterranean.

It had to be. If she had been in his shoes...ugh! There weren't enough pillows in the universe to drown out the voices in her head.

Returning to the empty bungalow had been the first time since he'd moved in that the little house by the sea hadn't felt like home. Without him, it felt dark and lifeless.

Sure enough, when she finally gave up thrashing around in her bed after a fractious sleep, she blindly made her way to the kitchen to turn on the coffeemaker, only to burst into tears.

Santi knew her every move. How could she not have noticed how—even with the separate bedrooms rule that suddenly seemed quaint and respectful rather than the snub she'd taken it as—she and Santi had become part of each other's lives?

She'd heat up the milk. He'd hand her the coffee. He'd flick on the morning news while she waited for the jolt of Café Cubano to make an impact on her droopy eyelids while he strode around achieving things like the able-bodied morning person he was. She'd driven the ambulance. He'd quizzed her on her coursework.

They had been a team.

The sharp tang of freshly brewed coffee became an acrid reminder that a caffeine hit was a no-no now. She decided to get a glass of juice from the refrigerator, only to lodge some grit under her foot. She scanned the open living space for her flip-flops.

It took a few minutes to track down the first one through the cloudy sheet of tears blocking her vision. The second one? Who knew?

Santi had always been the finder in this scenario. Her reliable other half who had made her whole and she had stupidly driven him away.

Her cell phone's distinctive ringtone broke into the morning silence. Her heart leaped for a moment. Santi?

She grabbed the phone from the countertop and stared at the digital display.

Amanda.

Her heart sank, but she forced herself to answer the phone with a cheery "Hello."

Destroying all her relationships was inadvisable at this juncture.

"Hey, you. What's up with the ambulance rescheduling?"

"What?" Saoirse felt her blood run cold. Santi might not have spent the night at the bungalow but she had still been clinging to the ridiculous hope she'd see him at work. That she'd have just one more chance to explain.

"I overheard one of the guys saying he was getting a new partner today. *You.*"

Her breath caught in her throat.

"Murphy?" Amanda drew out her name warily. "What's going on? Have you two had a fight?"

"Something like that," she mumbled.

How to explain the myriad complications? She was deeply regretting not speaking with Amanda before she'd come up with her brilliant plan to cut her losses with Santi before he found out about the baby. That's what friends were for, right? Talking you out of half-baked ideas.

"Well, go fix it," Amanda stated without reservation.

"It's not that easy."

"Yes, it is," Amanda retorted in her usual nononsense style. "Who cares if your pride takes a bit of a bashing? If you love him, it will be easy. And from all the crazy vibes you've been putting out into the universe, I have a feeling it will be easy."

"Nothing's that simple!"

I'm carrying his child.

"It is when you decide to stop fighting." Amanda's voice was suddenly drowned out with a surge of noise from the ER. "Gotta run. Go fix it, hun. Love ya. Bye!"

Saoirse dropped onto the sofa, as if physically letting her friend's words sink in.

Fighting *what*, exactly?

She gave her forehead a thud with the heel of her hand. Whether it was pregnancy or her trademark stubbornness, she was being a Class-A idiot.

She loved Santi and was actively sabotaging her relationship with him just to protect...

She growl-screamed in frustration at her idiocy.

To protect her heart.

She was no better than her ex who had cut and run when it had mattered the most. Apart from which, how on earth was she expecting to protect her heart from being broken by cutting to the chase and breaking it herself?

Hormones?

It was a handy catchall…but she was fairly certain she'd have to shoulder the blame on this one.

The pregnant woman's list of dos and don'ts was something Saoirse knew back to front from her training. What to eat. What not to eat. Physical risks. Sensible precautions. None of them covered affairs of the heart. Today she had a new advisory to add:

Warning: to all pregnant women who thought they were doing the right thing by ending it with the man they loved. You're being an idiot. Don't do it. Stick with the scary stuff. Take the risk.

Take the risk.

The words formed a loop in her head. Slowly at first, then gaining traction like a car on a racetrack. What was the worst that could happen? She'd get deported. Big deal. It wasn't about visas. Or borders. Or margaritas at Mad Ron's or even the beautiful sunrises and sunsets Miami seemed to specialize in. It was all about Santi and whether or not he was in her life. In *their* lives. She had to act for two now. And it was time to act courageously.

Take the risk.

"Thanks for pulling a double, Santiago. You've got me out of one helluva pickle. I've called just about everyone I can think of. You're sure you want the whole week?"

"Never met an overnight shift I didn't like," Santi replied with a grimness that actively contrasted with his chirpy proclamation. Sleep hadn't come easily the past couple of nights so he might as well try and do some good in the world.

"Great. I'll ink you in, then. You military guys..." The controller shook his head in admiration. "We're lucky to have you."

"Don't worry about it." Santi gave him a clap on the arm, grateful for the kind words. They restored a minuscule portion of the dignity he'd left behind when he'd lashed out at Saoirse the other night. Taking on a few extra shifts was the least he could do in the penance department. Not that she knew about it. He hadn't missed the fact that her name had disappeared from the roster sheets either.

"You happy to work with Rodriguez?"

"Very," he replied distractedly. He didn't have a clue who Rodriguez was. Didn't care, really.

Just as long as his partner wasn't Saoirse. Seeing her now would be torture. He might regret his behavior, but he didn't have it in him to apologize, to play the noble loser. Not with the cannon-sized wounds his heart was trying to cope with.

And yet he still had the damn ring in his pocket. Had carried it around with him for the past two days. Not to return. That could wait, too. He tugged the box out of his pocket to see if it would turn oracle when he flicked the lid open, and the diamond immediately caught the light.

A dazzler. Just like Saoirse had been the first time he'd laid eyes on her. First and last. Her light had never faded, only become brighter.

He snapped the lid shut and stuffed it back into the deep pockets of his regulation-issue cargo pants. Maybe he'd keep the ring as a cruel talisman to remind him what happened when you didn't enter into a relationship with all your senses on high alert.

No. That didn't sit right either. You didn't stop loving someone just because you didn't get what you wanted.

He thought of his brothers. The ease and love with which they'd opened up their hearts to him. Not a word of anger. No malice for the years he'd left them wondering. Just pure, straight-to-the-core, unconditional love.

Exactly what he felt for Saoirse.

It had just about killed him to hear her dismiss their time together as if it had been nothing.

So. Night shifts it was until he figured out how to find the best path to forgiveness.

He stared out of the huge ambulance garage into the night sky, his future opening up like an unfillable black hole. There would be no replacing Saoirse. That was a no-brainer. But forgiveness might help make moving on that little bit easier to bear. He could start up a poker game with his brothers. Four single Valentinos—maybe a couple of the other surgeons could join them. He might even consider taking a few shifts in the ER, shore up his emergency medicine skills. After all, the military had made a huge investment in him. He could fill the emptiness in his life with payback. Patient after patient. Life after life. Making a difference. Trying to do the best he could in the face of having messed it all up again.

"You Valentino?" A man in his early twenties holding a duffel bag was stretching out his hand.

"The one and only! Unless you add my brothers into the mix." He slapped a smile on his face and shook the man's hand. "I'm guessing you're Rodriguez."

"Samuel." He gave Santi's hand a firm shake and then dropped it as if he'd been stung. "*Cara-*

coles! Hang on a minute—are you one of *those* Valentinos?" Samuel gave a low whistle.

"I'm not strictly sure how to answer that. Are you saying it's a good or a bad thing?"

"Neither, man." He whistled again. "It's just... I was from the same neighborhood as you. My family used to go to your parents' bodega all the time. *Mi madre...*" He laughed warmly as the memory came to him. "After you all went through what you did, my mother used to use you boys as an example whenever I misbehaved. 'You don't see the Valentino brothers lying around, watching TV all day!

"'You should take a page out of the Valentino household and pick up a book and study!'"

Samuel's overexaggerated reenactment of his mother's admonishments made Santi chuckle.

"If she saw what we were really like she probably would have told you to steer well clear of us." None of them had been perfect. But they'd all worked hard and were doing their best to make a difference in the world.

"Eh, *bonco!*" Samuel put on a warning tone, though his face was wreathed in a warm smile. "Don't go telling me the reason I became a paramedic has no basis. Your family was the only reason I ever did any homework at all!"

"Glad to have helped," Santi said, meaning it from the bottom of his heart. He'd come home to find peace and be someone his brothers could be proud of. It gave him a swell of pride to hear they all had lent a hand in inspiring Sam.

"You go sort your stuff out and I'll get this baby loaded up." Santi pointed at their rig and turned toward the back to do his preliminary supplies check. He never relied on the previous crew, always had to check for himself they were stocked with everything they might need. "Self-contained at all times!" He heard Saoirse's voice as clear as a bell in his head. He had made her repeat it time after time when she'd leaped straight into the cab of the ambulance, cranked the engine and revved the vehicle to hit the road without checking. No point in going somewhere if you weren't prepared.

He thought he had been when he'd taken her out to the beach. Ring, beautiful woman he loved. Job done.

Talk about being blindsided.

"Sure thing, bro. I'll just go and dump my bag in the locker room and see you in a few. And be sure to tell your brothers from me, thank you."

"For what?"

"For making sure I kept on the right side of the tracks."

Santi waved off the compliment and lengthened his stride. It was nice to talk about his brothers without the usual hit of guilt.

He reached for the back door of the ambulance and clicked the handle open, thinking how lucky he was to have them. They would be keeping him on the straight and narrow now that—

"Hello, Santi."

An all-consuming stillness took hold of him. *Saoirse.*

"I'm about to go on shift."

"I know. That's why I asked Sam if I could wait here."

"Self-contained at all times," they repeated together, eyes locked.

"I don't know if this is a good idea. The other night was…" He faltered, unable to finish his train of thought as his gaze meshed with hers again. The connection was virtually palpable, his fingers aching all the while to reach out and touch her, stroke her soft-as-a-rose-petal cheek with the back of his hand. Her pink lips wore a gentle smile, her blue eyes, a bit red-rimmed, were wide with hope that he would hear her out.

He felt his chest heave and heavily huff out an indecisive sigh. The sooner he forgave her, the sooner he could move on.

His brothers had done it in milliseconds. Did he have the strength to do the same?

Dios! He hadn't even really pinpointed what he was forgiving her for.

Unwittingly breaking his heart? It wasn't as

if he'd opened up and told her how he'd felt. If anything, he'd been pushing her further away the deeper in love he'd become.

Saoirse climbed down from the interior bench and settled on the wide rear step of the ambulance, giving the step a little pat so that he would join her.

The least he could do was hear her out. Listening came first. The ring box jammed into his leg as he sat down so he stretched out his legs, feigning a nonchalance he didn't feel.

"I know I hijacked whatever it was you were going to say to me the other day," Saoirse began, both of their gazes fastidiously fixed on the stream of traffic flowing past them outside the EMT garage.

"That's one way of putting it."

If only you knew.

"I feel awful about the things I said."

"Then why did you say them?"

There was heat behind his words and Saoirse couldn't blame him. She deserved it. She'd made a foolish decision for an even more ridiculous reason. She sucked in a breath and kept going.

"I have no right to know what you were going to say to me the other day, but if I explain to you why I was such an impulsive idiot, would you tell me what you were going to say?"

Santi eyed her warily. He didn't answer, but he wasn't running for the hills or telling her to get out of his life, which she'd half braced herself for.

"Go on, then." His fingers drummed impatiently on the metal step.

It wasn't a promise but at least he'd hear her out. It was more than she felt she deserved.

"When I spoke to you the other day, just about everything I said was fear-based. I guess, because of what I went through back in Ireland, the last thing I ever wanted when you agreed to help me with my visa problems was to feel trapped. It's obvious that's what my ex felt and why he bolted, and I never wanted to go through that again. Everything I told you was true. I do want to live here. I do love the work. Working with you."

Loving you.

Santi's energy level shot up a notch. She sensed the hairs bristling at the nape of his neck as he turned to her and said, "You've got a funny way of showing it."

She nodded in agreement. "You're right. It's just that something happened to me—something *big*—and it threw me off balance. I've spoken to my manager, who thought it would best if I transferred off ambulances—"

"You're not sick, are you?" A jag of concern darkened Santi's features.

"No, no! Not at all. I feel great. I mean, I'm fine." She flopped her hands into her lap and shot him a hangdog look. "I—I'm not doing this very well, am I?" She grinned apologetically, hoping the smile encapsulated the deep love she felt for him. Dumping all her feelings into his lap and telling him about the miracle her body was celebrating seemed too much to unload on him in one hit but...

This could very well be her last chance.

She hesitated for a moment before carefully pulling a black-and-white photo from the envelope in her backpack and held it between them. The image would say more than she ever could.

The picture wasn't very clear.

Just a blur of grey lines in a large arc of blackness. She was only about seven weeks along so it was near impossible to make out the miniature fingers and toes their child was busily growing. Within its little peanut-sized body she had only just heard her baby's heartbeat—a heartbeat that would steadily build in strength. The tiny ear buds just beginning to form that would, in just a few short weeks, be able to discern between her voice and Santi's. If he chose to accept the olive branch she was offering. No expectations or demands...just understanding that she'd been trying her best.

The silence of his response was anything but passive.

The air between them virtually crackled with electricity. Tingles skittered along Saoirse's spine as Santi's dark, black-lashed eyes took in the image, the gold flecks catching alight as the meaning of the scan took hold.

Her eyes followed his across the top of the scan, where her name was printed along with a couple of small hand-scribbled notes about conception date…expected due date…the teensy-tiny measurements. A pea? A plump blueberry at a stretch…

His eyes flicked to hers and she saw what she had barely dared to hope for. Love. Compassion. And wonder.

"Looks tall."

"He takes after his father." She tried to answer as neutrally as she could.

Santi's eyebrows shot up.

"Or she," Saoirse quickly filled in.

"Too early to tell," they said at the same time, their eyes catching as their voices wove together then faded into nervy laughs.

Santi took hold of the image and held it up between them again. "I hope you don't think for a second you're raising this baby on your own."

His words may have been stern but they were more than Saoirse had hoped to hear. Tears stung at the back of her throat as she tried to keep her emotions in check. This was just the first step.

"I was—"

"I was—"

They both began to talk at the same time, chasing up their snafus with "Go ahead" and "No, you first" until Saoirse finally dissolved into nervous giggles, rose from the bumper and gave a curtsy with the billowing skirts of an imaginary ball gown. "Please, good sir, I insist you go first."

Santi's mind worked at lightning speed, trying to unravel the tangle of questions he had. They struck him in electric shots of understanding, all leading to the same realization. He was going to be a *father*.

"How?"

Hardly elegant, but it covered all the bases.

"The doctors aren't really sure," Saoirse began, the bright sparks of delight lighting her up from within. "I showed them all my medical history from Ireland and they reckon my doctor there shouldn't have been so absolute in pronouncing me infertile." She flushed a little and shot him a shy glance. "They say sometimes what doesn't work with one person does with another. It's just a question of finding the best match."

"And I'm that match?" he asked before his brain caught up with his mouth.

"Looks like it." Saoirse nodded, hands clasped tightly in her lap. "Would you like to keep the photo? I can get more to you as the baby grows."

"What do you mean, get more to me?" Santi tried to temper the disbelief in his voice. "I'm coming with you to the next scan. And the one after that."

"Oh, Santi, that's so nice—but you've already been so kind to me—"

He put a hand up and she stopped, lips parted, in midflow. The most beautiful woman he'd ever seen and now she was carrying his *child*. He wouldn't have expected to feel an instant kinship to the little black-and-white bean in the scan and yet? His heart was near to bursting with joy.

"*Dulzera*…let me stop you there. It's my turn now and let me assure you, nothing about this moment is about being *kind* or *nice* or *polite*. This is about what I feel for you. *Have been* feeling for you over the past few weeks. More to the point, this is about what I wanted to say to you the other night, but should have said weeks ago after I set things right with my brothers."

Now it was Saoirse's turn to look bewildered. All the time he'd spent with his brothers—time he'd spent keeping her at arm's length—had been precisely what had led her to believe he deserved to be freed from their arrangement. Her eyes flitted across his face as if his cheekbones, his eyes, the aquiline strength of his nose would spell it all out for her. His mouth was so beautiful. Too bad her brain was buzzing so much she couldn't make out what he was saying. She scrunched her eyebrows together and made a concerted effort to tune into that chocolaty voice of his.

"I was going to ask you if you really wanted to get married, but—"

"You *were* going to ask me to marry you?" Saoirse bolted upright. "What happened?"

Santi threw back his head and laughed a full-bodied guffaw.

"Would you be patient for once, *cariño*? I was trying to explain to you what happened when you were busy dumping me."

"I wasn't dumping you," Saoirse protested. "I was *rescuing* you from being trapped in a marriage you didn't want to be in."

"Well, what if I didn't want rescuing?" Santi parried as he, too, rose from the ambulance step.

She froze—gaze glued on his chest—too afraid to look up into those gold-flecked eyes of his.

She watched Santi's hand slip into the front pocket of his cargos and pull out a... Oh-h-h-h... an eggshell-blue box. Her heart was beating so hard she could virtually see it thumping through her top.

With a single fluid move he flicked open the box so she could see the most beautiful ring that had probably ever been made.

"Saoirse Murphy?"

"You said it perfectly!"

Saoirse's fingers fluttered to cover her mouth. She could hardly believe her eyes. The man who'd woven himself into her heart was dropping to one knee.

"You were right about one thing," Santi began, a smile tugging at the corners of his mouth. "I didn't want to marry you so you could get your green card. I wanted to marry you because I loved you—*do* love you. I love you with all my heart and hope that you will do me the honor of becoming my wife."

"Are you sure? I mean, I don't want to find all your brothers showing up at the wedding with shotguns at your back or any—"

"For heaven's sake, Murph! I didn't know until just now that you were pregnant. You're really going to put me through my paces, aren't you?"

Her face morphed into a hugely apologetic wince before splitting into an enormous smile as she threw herself at him.

"I just want you to be sure. You seemed so happy that you had sorted everything with your brothers and the happier you were, the less time you spent with me."

"It's because I didn't want them to meet you—"

"Ha! I knew it." Saoirse's fists landed triumphantly on her hips after jabbing a triumphant finger into the air.

"Murphy!" Santi threw his own hands into the air, nearly losing the ring in the process. They both lurched forward to check it was still nestled in the pillow of satin. Santi took advantage of the proximity and took Saoirse's hands in one of his own, a finger of the other resting across her lips. "Will you keep your gift of the gab to yourself just this once so I can finish?"

Saoirse nodded obediently.

"I didn't want to introduce you to my brothers as my fake wife. I wanted to introduce you to them as my fiancée. My real fiancée. Or girlfriend. There's no rush."

"Well, there is a bit of a rush actually—"

"For heaven's sake, woman!" Santi stood up, scooping Saoirse into his arms as he did. "There's only one way to keep you quiet, isn't there?"

"What's that?" Saoirse asked, semi-innocently.

"Like this." He lowered his lips to hers, gently at first, then intensifying with need and a growing hunger for more as Saoirse responded in kind. The weeks of pent-up desire took flight in their kisses, each one building in passion and intent.

"Can I take the fact that you're in my arms to be a yes?" Santi murmured after a few moments, his lips whispering against her own.

"Absolutely, it's a yes," Saoirse replied, leaning in for yet another life-affirming connection with...she could hardly believe it...her husband-to-be.

"What the—"

Saoirse felt Santiago's lips leave her own before she put two and two together. They had an audience.

"Murph." Santiago put her back down on the ground. "I think you've already met my shift partner, Samuel Rodriguez. Samuel, I'd like you to meet my fiancée, Saoirse."

Saoirse put out her hand with an embarrassed grin. "Murphy's fine."

For the second time that night Rodriguez let out a low, impressed whistle.

"Not for long, though, is it?" Santi slipped an arm around his bride-to-be's waist.

"What do you mean?" Saoirse looked up at him, her face wreathed in smiles.

"Come St. Patrick's Day," he said with a leading grin, "it'll be Valentino."

* * * * *

Look out for the next great story in the
HOT LATIN DOCS *quartet*

ALEJANDRO'S SEXY SECRET
by Amy Ruttan

*And there are two more fabulous stories to
come!*

*If you enjoyed this story, check out these
other great reads from Annie O'Neil*

*THE NIGHTSHIFT BEFORE CHRISTMAS
ONE NIGHT, TWIN CONSEQUENCES*